Faith *and* Drama

Plays and Readings from a Biblical Perspective

Montana Lattin

Copyright © 2018 by Montana Lattin.
Cover art by Cindy Kopenhafer

HARDBACK: 978-1-948779-72-2
PAPERBACK: 978-1-948779-71-5
EBOOK: 978-1-948779-73-9

All rights reserved. No part of this publication may be reproduced, distributed, or transmitted in any form or by any electronic or mechanical means, without the prior written permission of the publisher, except in the case of brief quotations embodied in critical reviews and certain other noncommercial uses permitted by copyright law.

Ordering Information:

For orders and inquiries, please contact:
1-888-375-9818
www.toplinkpublishing.com
bookorder@toplinkpublishing.com

Printed in the United States of America

Contents

KINGDOM LIFE
    Grumbling over Coffee 3
    Rest in Me 9
    Body of Christ 13
    Born Again 18
    The Freedom of Obedience 23
    The First Will Be Last 27
    The Way of Mercy 31
    No Other Gods 36
    Our Father 40
    Love 44
    Joy 48
    Peace 55
    Patience 59
    Goodness 65
    Faithfulness 71
    Gentleness 75

CHRISTMAS
    Homeless 81
    Joseph's Dream 93
    The Gift 97
    The Hope of All the World 102
    Waiting with a Promise 107
    Breakable God 113
    Behold 120

EASTER
Peter 127
Unexpected Love 132
Jesus' Dream...137
Water and Wind 142
Sacrifice 147

READINGS
The Sower..155
Lazarus and the Rich Man..162
In the Shadow of His Wings 167
Prayers from the Kingdom 171
Prophecies and Promises 176
O, Sovereign Lord..182
The Shepherd King..187

KINGDOM LIFE

Grumbling over Coffee

Characters
Whiner
Martyr
Cynic
Perfectionist
Owner
Waiter

Running time: 5 minutes

Setting
Four customers sitting at a table in a cafe. Each character who is a customer may wear a t-shirt with their name on it. For example, "Whiner".

Whiner: Why is it always so hot in here? It's unbearable!

Perfectionist: It's either too hot or too cold, it's never just right.

Cynic: And it never will be, so just get used to it.

Martyr: If *you're* uncomfortable, imagine how *I* feel! I'm the one with health problems.

Whiner: You're such a martyr! You always think everything is worse for you.

Martyr: That's because it is! Whiner!

Whiner: I don't whine! (*In a whiney voice…*) When is our coffee going to come? We've been waiting forever.

Cynic: What difference does it make? It's never good anyway.

Perfectionist: It's either too hot or too cold. No matter how many times you send it back, they never get it right!

The waiter brings the coffee and puts it down.

Whiner: It's about time!

Martyr: *(Takes a sip.)* Ow! I burned my mouth! They did that on purpose!

Cynic: Of course they did! It figures!

Waiter: No! I, …I mean, so sorry!

The waiter quickly walks down stage right. The owner reads a newspaper.

Waiter: Wow, those people complain a lot!

Owner: You noticed that, huh? Unfortunately, that's the way they are about everything.

Waiter: How can they stand being like that?

Owner: A complainer never thinks they are one—they only see it in other people!

Perfectionist: *(Drinks his coffee.)* Is this the best they can do? I'm telling you, people are lazy. They just don't care.

Cynic: What do you expect? It's human nature!

Martyr: I could tell them how to make really good coffee, but what's the point? They wouldn't appreciate it.

Whiner: These chairs are so uncomfortable. My back is killing me!

The scene shifts back to the Owner and Waiter.

Waiter: Why do they come here every day if everything is so terrible?

Owner: Oh, they're waiting for something. The Lord God of the universe has a party that everyone is invited to. They're waiting to be let in.

Waiter: But they're never invited in. Is that because...

Owner: Yeah. Complainers don't enter the Kingdom of Heaven.

Waiter: Wow, that's serious!

Owner: That's the problem. They won't admit how serious their complaining is. But to God, it's very serious. At the root of complaining is a heart of unbelief.

Waiter: You mean they don't believe in God?

Owner: Oh, they believe in him. They just don't believe that he can and will bring good out of evil.

Waiter: *(Thinking...)* Well, He *is* the one who's ultimately in control of everything!

Owner: Right. What's the point of believing in him if we don't trust him?

Waiter: I see. Wow, *I* need to stop complaining!

Whiner: I'm tired of coming here every day! When do we get to go in to the party?

Martyr: Probably never! People like us never get invited to anything fun.

Cynic: Of course not. It'll never change.

Whiner: Excuse me! Waiter! *(The waiter comes over.)*

Perfectionist: What can he do, he's just the waiter! *(To the waiter.)* We'd like to speak to the manager!

Waiter: I'll get him. *(Signals the owner to come over.)*

Cynic: *(To the Perfectionist.)* You're so naive! It won't change anything!

Whiner: *(To the Owner.)* Look, we come here every day but we never get into the party. What's going on?

Martyr: Everyone else gets to enter! Everyone but us.

Owner: Only the Lord God of the universe decides who goes in.

Perfectionist: But why does he make people wait?

Owner: Actually, *He's* the one who's waiting for something.

Cynic: Of course! Nothing's ever simple!

Perfectionist: We're always here on time. What more does he want?

Owner: He wants you to remember why you're here on this earth—to be light in a dark world. You can't do that and complain about everything at the same time.

Whiner: It's just a way of letting off steam. So we complain about little things here and there. It's not that big a deal!

Owner: He sees it as a kind of rebellion.

Whiner: But surely God knows that living in this world is hard! We deserve better!

Owner: Jesus wouldn't have had to die if you deserved better. But he did die and he took the punishment you deserve.

Martyr: Well, ...it's true. It could be so much worse! I focus on the negative so much I'm not nearly as grateful as I should be.

Cynic: And if I'm honest with myself, maybe I really *don't* believe God is in control of everything!

Perfectionist: I know he's in control. I just can't help thinking I could do a better job. ...I guess that *is* rebellion!

Cynic: For both of us!

Whiner: I have been told my whining makes everything worse. It even makes me feel worse, so it's probably true.

Martyr: What if all the complaining were to stop right now? We'd be completely different people!

Cynic: Even I have to admit that with God's help, it is possible to change.

The waiter walks up and hands the Owner a note. He reads it to himself.

Owner: My friends, the door is now open. Please join the party of the Lord God of the Universe.

Perfectionist: Already?!

Owner: Of course! You don't have to be perfect to enter!

Perfectionist: *(Humbly.)* Oh, well, that's good news!

Music plays. The Waiter holds open the door while they happily enter the party.

Music fades.

Rest in Me

Characters
Jesus
Laurie
Neighbor

Running time: 3 minutes

Setting
A woman sits on a suitcase upstage center. She is loaded down with a large suitcase and duffle bags. Her neighbor walks by carrying a bag.

Neighbor: Hi neighbor! Why are you sitting here all alone?

Laurie: Just thinking.

Neighbor: Thinking? In the middle of the sidewalk? You always were a strange one. *(Hands her a bag, which Laurie takes without thinking. Exits.)*

Laurie: Strange? *(Pause.)* Great! Do all the neighbors think I'm strange?

Jesus enters down stage left.

Jesus: Hi Laurie. How are you?

Laurie: *(Depressed.)* Oh, hi Jesus. I'm fine.

Jesus: Really? I haven't seen you with this much baggage since we first met. *(She ignores him.)* Well, if you don't feel like talking. *(Leaves)*

Laurie: No, wait! Jesus, please wait up. *(With great effort she gathers everything and comes after him.)* I need you!

Jesus: Laurie, what are you doing? Remember what I said to you on the day we met?

Laurie: You said, "Come to me you who are weary and heavy burdened and I will give you rest."

Jesus: Exactly! You came to me and I took all your burdens. What happened?

Laurie: Life is hard!

Jesus: No one knows that better than me. If someone told you it was going to be easy, they were lying.

Laurie: But you also promised an abundant life!

Jesus: An abundant life is not the same as an easy life. Easier is not better.

Laurie: Okay, but why's it so hard for me and so easy for other people?

Jesus: It's not. That's a lie. No wonder you carry around so much stuff.

Laurie: But I have to carry it, don't I? What exactly is this stuff?

Jesus: It's every bad thing that anyone's ever said or done to you. Plus a lot of lies you've told yourself.

Laurie: I'm so tired, Jesus! Can you help me find rest again? *(Jesus picks up the bag the neighbor left.)* My neighbor just said I was strange.

Jesus: You care more about what your neighbor thinks of you than what I think?

He throws the bag off the front of the stage. With each piece of luggage he throws away, she feels noticeably lighter. He picks up another one.

Laurie: My dad said I wasn't as pretty as my sister.

Jesus: That was ten years ago!

Laurie: Really? It feels like yesterday.

Jesus: *(He throws the bag offstage.)* As long as you try to get your self worth from other people you'll never be free. You are my unique and beautiful princess. I love you inside and out. Do you believe me? *(She nods. He picks up another.)* And this?

Laurie: My best friend lied to my face.

Jesus: That's extremely hurtful. People will let you down. What do you do—with my help?

Laurie: Forgive her, the way you forgave me? *(Jesus throws the bag off the stage.)*

Jesus: Speaking of sins.... *(Holds up another bag.)*

Laurie: That's me feeling guilty about my sins.

Jesus: I took care of that! *(Throws it off stage.)* You no longer have to live in guilt and fear.

Laurie: (*Feeling lighter with each piece he has taken*) Yeah, I think I see what you mean. Here! Please take this... (*She pushes the last large suitcase toward Jesus. He throws it off the stage.*) What a relief! I feel... *hopeful* again. Thank you!

Jesus: Now, I'm going to give you one thing to carry.

Laurie: What's that?

Jesus: *(He touches her forehead.)* The Truth. Keep it here, pull it out when you need it, and you'll never pick up another piece of useless baggage again.

Laurie: Right! Wow! Was my pride in that suitcase? I feel so much lighter, so... free!

Jesus: All my children are free. They just have to get used to living that way!

They exit.

Body of Christ

Characters
John
Bete
Mark
Ree

Running time: 3 minutes

Setting
John sits alone on a park bench and reads aloud from the Bible.

John: *(Reads.)* "And let us not neglect our meeting together, as some people do, but encourage one another, especially now that the day of his return is drawing near."* *(Talks out loud to himself.)* Wow, Lord, everything I read lately is about the body of Christ and being part of a community. I'm starting to feel bad about not belonging to any church right now. *(Prays.)* Father, I want to obey you on this. Please help me. Just tell me where you want me to go. In Jesus' name, Amen. *(Continues reading the Bible silently. Bete enters.)*

Bete: Hi! Sorry to interrupt but I see you're reading the Bible!

John: Yes...

Bete: I think that's great! My name is Bete.

John: John.

Bete: Nice to meet you. Actually, there's a Bible study tonight at my church! Would you like to come?

John: That's amazing! I was just praying that God would show me a church to join!

Bete: I love the way he answers prayer! So, you'll come?

John: Where is it?

Bete: We meet at the place near the square.

John: Oh, uh, no, actually I can't come.

Bete: Really? Why?

John: Well, no offense but I've been there before.

Bete: And...?

John: Well... it was kind of boring. The worship was very quiet. Plus it's pretty far from my house.

Bete: Have you been to the church on the other side, then? The one closer to here?

John: I have, actually. The worship there is too wild, too much waving of the arms and yelling—just the opposite problem.

Bete: Oh. Oh well, if you change your mind. Bye!

John: Bye! *(Continues reading.)*

Bete exits stage left but stops to check her phone for a text.

Mark: Hi John, how are you?

John: Good! How's it going?

Mark: Was that Bete I saw you talking to just now?

John: Yeah. She was telling me about her Bible study. I'm looking for a church to join.

Mark: Oh, why don't you come to the Riverside church? We haven't seen you in, wow, at least two years now.

John: No way.

Mark: Why not?

John: I don't want to gossip so I can't really talk about it. But let's just say someone said something that really wasn't cool and I'm not going back until I get an apology.

Mark: I'm sorry to hear that. Did you talk to them about it?

John looks at Mark like, "You're kidding, right?"

Mark: That's too bad. Anyway, I'm going to catch up with Bete. See you later!

John: See you!

Ree: Hi John, what's going on? *(Sees Bible.)* Oh, you're reading the Bible.

John: Yeah, everything I read or listen to lately tells me that being a Christian means being in community.

Ree: That sounds true for so many reasons. We are called the *body* of Christ after all! So what's the problem?

John: I'm asking God to lead me to the right church, but nothing's come up yet.

Ree: Oh, well how about the church on the west side?

John: I went there for about six months. Then I got sick and the pastor didn't come to visit me even once.

Ree: Oh, I see! The church at the top of the hill then?

John: The worship director's a control freak! I just can't get along with someone like that.

Ree: The church across the river?

John: That church is full of hypocrites. In fact I'm beginning to remember why I stopped going to church. They're all full of hypocrites!

Ree: Huh. Okay. Well, I see Mark and Bete over there. I'll catch up with you later!

John: *(Talks out loud to God.)* Wow, Lord, I didn't know this was going to be so hard. You really aren't showing me any place! *(He returns to reading.)*

After a few moments Mark, Ree and Bete come by all talking excitedly together.

Mark: Hey, John, we just decided to have a prayer time together. Would you like to join us?

John: Oh, no thanks!

The group continues to move off stage. Ree returns.

Ree: *(Speaks kindly.)* You know, John, none of us is perfect. And church isn't about us anyway. It's about God. *(She exits.)*

John: I know that! *(After a moment.)* Well, Father, I want to obey you in this. But I guess I'll just have to wait until I find a church with no hypocrites!

John closes his Bible and exits.

---

*Hebrews 10:25

Born Again

Characters
Researcher 1
Researcher 2
Nicodemus
Mary

Running time: 3 minutes

Setting
Two researchers in a lab wearing white coats and holding clipboards take notes.

Researcher 1: If we want to know what this "born again" thing is it's important that we ask the right questions.

Researcher 2: Of course. I'll take notes. (*Writes.*) *Born Again*... what is it?

Researcher 1: Perhaps we should start by asking who it is for.

Researcher 2: Popular opinion is that the term "born again" applies to uneducated people who are emotional and needy.

Researcher 1: Right. That's why these two are here.

Researcher 2: *(Looks at his notes.)* This woman, Mary, has a very bad history indeed. She seems to fit the stereotype; poor, uneducated and gullible. *(To Mary.)* No offense. *(She shrugs.)*

Researcher 1: Yes. And this man, Nicodemus, is the opposite. He's a religious leader; highly educated, successful and respected.

Nicodemus: And yet... *(On hearing him speak, both researchers are startled.)*

Researcher 2: Wow that scared me!

Nicodemus: Did you think we were just going to sit here like a couple of dummies? *And yet*, even I could not enter the kingdom of heaven without being born again.

Researcher 1: So, you were a religious leader but not a good person?

Nicodemus: No, I was a good person. And very proud of it.

Mary: *(To Nicodemus.)* They're making the common mistake; they think being born again is about becoming a better person.

Nicodemus: *(Nods.)* You should know that being born again is about much more than just improved behavior—it's about God's own life being implanted in you.

Researcher 1: Oh! Write that down.

Researcher 2: *(Writes.) God's own life being implanted in you.*

Researcher 1: Sounds powerful. But answer this, how did you feel being told by Jesus that you needed God as much as this woman. *(To Mary.)* No offense.

Mary: Hey, so I was the lucky one! I already knew I couldn't save myself.

Nicodemus: I thought I could! My life was steeped in morality, tradition and religion. But Jesus challenged all of that.

Researcher 1: Well, this is confusing. So it's not about becoming more religious?

Nicodemus: No. Write this down: it's called "born again" because you receive a completely new identity. You become spiritually alive.

Researcher 2: Spiritually alive...?

Mary: You're able to sense spiritual realities that you couldn't sense before. It's like seeing through a completely new pair of eyes.

Researcher 1: What's one thing you see now that you didn't see before?

Mary: That's easy. I see God. I see what he has done for me out of love. His love has become so real that now I can handle anything that happens in this life. He is my life.

Researcher 2: And yet you admit you still have problems? You still struggle like everybody else?

Nicodemus: Of course. But before we were fighting a battle we could not win. Now we're fighting a battle we cannot lose. I watched him die on that cross, and later when he rose from the dead, I understood that he was making this new life possible. This is what he was trying to explain to me. He tried to tell me, but I... Excuse me.

Nicodemus becomes emotional remembering Jesus. He excuses himself and leaves the stage. Mary also gets up to leave.

Faith and Drama

Researcher 1: One more thing, you also became a respected person in your community. The changes in your life are obvious, but how has he changed?

Mary: You must have it in your records that when Nicodemus first came to see Jesus he came at night.

Researcher 2: Yes, we knew that.

Mary: Later, when Jesus died, everyone who knew him ran away out of fear. But Nicodemus had the courage to ask Pilate for his body.

Researcher 2: Well, yes, that is a big change from meeting Jesus in secret.

Mary: Yes, but that's not all. Nicodemus brought spices and linen with him. He washed Jesus' body and prepared it for burial.

Researcher 1: Ah, I see what you mean.

Researcher 2: I don't. So what?

Researcher 1: Normally only women and slaves did that kind of work. It was considered too menial and degrading for a man to do, especially a man like Nicodemus.

Researcher 2: Oh, I see. I think.

Researcher 1: Write this down: he not only became a person of courage, but his male pride, cultural pride, and class pride were gone. Because of his relationship with Jesus he became bolder—*and* more humble!

Researcher 2: Wow, it's like his whole identity had been pulled up and replanted.

Mary: Yes. He was born again!

Researchers 1 and 2: Aaah!

The Freedom of Obedience

Characters
Alice
Beth
David
Jesus

Running time: 2 minutes

Setting
Jesus and David are on stage. Alice enters trying to make a phone call using a banana.

Alice: Hello! Donna? Hellooo! Anybody there? Pick up!

David: Alice, what are you doing?

Alice: I'm trying to call Donna but I can't hear anything. Hmm. Let me try outside. *(She exits. Meanwhile Beth crosses the stage looking into a compact mirror and combing her hair with a ladle.)*

Beth: *(After a few moments.)* This isn't helping at all! Oh, forget it! *(Exits.)*

David: What's happening, Jesus? Has everyone gone crazy?

Jesus: What do you mean?

David: What do I mean? Look at what they're doing! (*Jesus shrugs.*) Alice was trying to make a phone call with a banana and Beth is combing her hair with a spoon!

Jesus says nothing.

David: They're not using things for what they were designed for!

Jesus: That's true. So... what do you think *your* design is?

David: You mean my skills?

Jesus: No.

David: My talents?

Jesus: No.

David: My dreams?

Beth enters holding a Mac Air laptop and waving a flyswatter back and forth in the air.

Beth: I can't connect to the internet at all with this thing!

David: *(To Beth)* Maybe because a flyswatter has nothing to do with the internet! *(She shrugs and exits. To Jesus.)* Oh! You mean what's *our* design. What did God design us humans for?

Jesus: Everything was created with a design in mind.

David: Um, I'm not sure...

Jesus: Humans were made for intimacy with God.

David: Does a user manual come with that?

Jesus: Yes, actually! That would be the Ten Commandments.

David: Oh! Of course. Ten rules we're supposed to live by.

Jesus: You can call them rules. Or you can call them by what they represent; love, honor, integrity... The point is, they help you live out your design in perfect freedom.

David: Freedom? Can you have rules and be free at the same time?

Alice walks in very depressed with something in a napkin.

David: What's that?

Alice: It's my fish. I wanted him to be free. But when I freed him from his fish bowl he just flopped around on the ground and then died! *(Exits. David just looks at Jesus. Then..)*

David: Hmm. I'm beginning to understand how important this is. The way to intimacy with God—and ultimate freedom—is to fulfill our design.

Alice comes running back onstage.

Alice: Hey, my fish wasn't dead! I threw him back in the water and he revived! He's full of life again and swimming around like crazy! Isn't that great? *(Exits.)*

David: Yeah, great! *(To Jesus.)* Lesson learned! Given a choice, I think I'd rather swim in the ocean of God's love than flop around on the ground!

They exit.

The First Will Be Last

Characters
Doorman
Robert
Woman (or Man)

Running time 2-3 minutes

The doorkeeper stands center stage. An old woman (or man) with a cane slowly makes her way toward the entrance.

Doorkeeper: *(To the woman...)* Greetings! Welcome to the Kingdom of God!

Woman: Oh, yes! Greetings to you! Thank you, thank you so much!

Robert enters, rushes past her kicking the cane from under her causing her to fall.

Doorkeeper: *(Helps the woman to a seat.)* Oh!! Are you alright?

Woman: *(Shaken)* Oh, uh …yes, I think so! I was just coming when that gentleman…

Robert: Oh! Am I responsible for that? So, sorry! I didn't even notice. My mistake.

Doorkeeper: I see. Well, I think this woman was before you. If you'd like to wait?

Robert: (*Clearing up a misunderstanding*) Oh, no, I'm not a parishioner! I mean I'm not just a parishioner. (*To woman*) You remember me. (*To Doorkeeper*) I'm Robert. I run the senior citizens free lunch program …among other things.

Doorman: Okay, Robert. What's in your hand? (*One hand is tightly closed in a fist*)

Robert: Oh, that just happened over time. I can't seem to open it. I'm sure that can be fixed once I get inside.

Doorman: You seem pretty sure you'll get inside.

Robert: Well, …of course. I've always worked very hard! Ask anyone, I have a good reputation in my community.

Doorman: Yes, actually that's what you're holding onto in your closed fist. Your reputation. And what else?

Robert: What do you mean?

Doorman: There's pain there too, other people's pain. You've caused some injury along the way.

Robert: Look, if there's been offense, it wasn't my intention! I've done my best!

Doorman: The best for you. I'm sorry, but in order to enter this Kingdom both hands must be open …and empty.

Robert: Seriously? *(Robert tries to open his hand but it won't open.)* I thought I had control over this but it's not opening.

Doorman: Here's more bad news. Sin, like all disease, spreads. Your sin has spread from your hand to your heart and eyes.

Robert: That can't be! Ask the people in my church! They would never believe it!

Doorman: You do a lot for the church.

Robert: Yes! Everyone knows my name!

Doorman: Do you know this woman's name? *(Pause)* I'm sorry, but knowing *where* the entrance is, is not enough. You can't come in.

Robert: But there must be something I can do!

Doorman: It would be better for you if you cut off your hand.

Robert: What? You're kidding? That's a little extreme! Is it really that important?

Doorman: It's not an option.

Robert continues trying to open his hand but it won't open.

Robert: Okay, I'll cut it off! I don't want this to keep spreading. Just tell me how!

Doorman: Repent! That is, if you think you need to.

Robert: *(Gives up trying to open hand)* No, I know you're right. I felt small and selfish as soon as I got close to the entrance.

Doorman: You really do need to talk to God.

Robert: Yes, I know. I know you're right. (*Confesses with difficulty*) Lord God, I confess I do love the attention of being in charge. When people listen to me, I feel powerful. I'm addicted to being needed. The truth is, while pretending to be a servant, I was really only serving myself. This is the opposite of what you taught us by example. (*Pause*) I am not the savior, Jesus. Only you are. I am so sorry. Please forgive me…

Robert's hand slowly opens. He shows joy and relief over this. Looks to heaven and exclaims:

Thank you, Lord! Thank you, Father! (*Turns to woman…*) I'm sorry, what's your name?

Woman: Miriam.

Robert: Miriam, you were coming in before me. Here, let me help you. (*He assists her to stand*) Go ahead!

Doorman: But surely she's not as important as you, Robert! She has the spirit of a child!

Robert: Then she's better than me! I don't deserve to go in at all!

Doorman: The Savior is waiting! And He knows you both by name! Welcome to the Kingdom of God!

The Woman takes Robert's arm and they enter together.

The Way of Mercy

Characters
Micah
Abe
Caleb
Man
Luke

Running time: 3-4 minutes

Setting
Lighting is dim. Eerie music plays. The four characters are spread out around the stage. A bruised Man is laying unconscious center stage. Each character debates with his conscience. Music fades.

Micah: Just tell me what to do! *(Looks around. Speaks to no one in particular.)* Just tell me! Tell me what I should do!

Luke: Who am I to help him? I don't even know him!

Caleb: It's not safe anyway! This makes me very nervous. I'm afraid for my life here.

Abe: I can see that he needs help but if I stop, then what? It turns into a whole thing!

Luke: I know one thing for certain; this man is not one of us!

Micah: No, he isn't....

Abe: If the tables were turned and it was me lying there instead of him, he certainly wouldn't help me.

Caleb: How do we know the people who did that to him aren't still around?

Luke: Anyway, he must have done something to bring this on himself. He should've been more careful! (*They slowly exit stage left. Only Micah remains.*)

Micah: (*Reflects out loud, his back to the injured man.*) I'm a good person. I keep the law—the law of my conscience mostly. Isn't that good enough?

The injured man, who is upstage from Micah, slowly sits up and speaks. Micah responds without turning around, as if he is having a conversation with his own conscience.

Man/Jesus: Then what are you worried about? Why don't you just leave?

Micah: (*Repeats.*) I'm a good person!

Jesus: And...?

Micah: I want to inherit eternal life. I don't want to do anything wrong; but this... *this* is asking too much!

Jesus: What does the law say? How do you read it?

Micah: "Love the Lord your God with all your heart, and with all your soul, and with all your strength, and with all your mind; and your neighbor as yourself."

Jesus: Then you know what to do!

Micah: But who *is* my neighbor?

Jesus: *(Stands slowly.)* You mean, who will become your neighbor?

Micah: See—this is too hard! I need clarification!

Jesus: If you were to do all you could to help an enemy, wouldn't he become your neighbor?

Micah: There are reasons why I can't do that!

Jesus: I see. The problem is not the law; the problem is that you can't keep the law.

Micah: *(Turns and looks at Jesus.)* Who are you?

Jesus: My name is Jesus.

Micah: And you keep the law perfectly, I suppose?

Jesus: I love God perfectly so I see my neighbor in every enemy.

Micah: To love God, to love my enemy. It feels like the same thing. I mean, I can't seem to do either.

Jesus: No, you're going to fail. But then what child doesn't?

Micah: Child...?

Jesus: You said you want to inherit eternal life. An inheritance can't be earned. It's a gift, isn't it, from parent to child? It's based on who you are, not what you do.

Micah: But that would make God my father.

Jesus: And you his son.

Micah: But then he really could ask anything of me!

Jesus: Yes. Anything.

Micah: I don't think... I mean, I can't make that commitment.

Jesus: You wouldn't be doing it alone.

Micah: No. It's too hard, and a little scary. See, I can't do it! But then what will become of me? I am a good person, really. Especially compared to other people! Oh, I feel sick...

During this, Micah lies down where Jesus had been lying. In effect, they have traded places. Jesus kneels down to comfort Micah. The others return.

Luke: *(To Jesus.)* It's good to be merciful but think about it. If you make a commitment to this man it will be a burden in more ways than one; your time, your money, your safety...

Abe: Even if you took him someplace for treatment and he got well, he'd only be sold into slavery when he couldn't pay his bills. It will all be for nothing!

Caleb: Not to mention, you're a hated outsider here. The people in town will assume *you* did this to him.

Luke: They won't believe you were trying to help—they'll most certainly put you to death!

Caleb: *(As they exit.)* Did you hear? They'll put you to death!

Micah: Lord, will you help me, even though I wouldn't help you?

Jesus: Yes.

Micah: But why? Why would you...

Jesus: I will help you. And you need to know that I won't stop helping you until you're completely well—no matter what the cost.

Lights fade out.

No Other Gods

Characters
Lukas
Jesus
Work / Old Man
Entertainment
Lisa

Running time: 2-3 minutes

Setting
Jesus and Lukas enter, they are in the middle of a conversation.

Lukas: It's such a relief to talk to you, Jesus! I have so many problems right now!

Jesus: I know. "Troubles multiply for those who chase after other gods."*

Lukas: Sorry, what? What does that mean?

Jesus: I don't think you even see me when you pray. There's no praise, only requests.

Lukas: It's hard to be full of praise when things are going wrong all the time!

Jesus: Maybe I can help with that by reminding you of the first commandment. "You shall have no other gods before me."

Lukas: I don't. Do I?

Jesus: Actually, yes. I'd like you to meet some of your other gods. Here's one of them. *(A very anxious person enters with a sign around his neck that reads, "Work".)*

Lukas: Really? But working hard at my job is a good thing, isn't it?

Jesus: Of course it is! Most of the time a false god starts out as something good. But when a good thing becomes the ultimate thing you care about, then it becomes an idol.

Lukas: Oh, when it becomes more important than God, you mean?

Jesus: Exactly. For example, what happens when you fail God?

Lukas: Well, if I repent, he forgives me—because he loves me unconditionally.

Jesus: Your job does not love you unconditionally. When you make an idol out of your job, or anything else, it will curse you when you fail.

Lukas: That's exactly what it feels like! When things go wrong, I feel like a worthless human being!

Jesus: If God is your real Savior, your sense of worth won't depend on how well you do.

"Work" exits and person wearing the "Entertainment" sign enters. "Entertainment" never stops playing with his cell phone the whole time.

Lukas: Oh yeah. I spend a lot of time online.

Jesus: *A lot* of time? If your friend Lisa spent all her time with Charlie and rarely saw you, what would that tell you?

Lukas: That she cared more for Charlie than for me.

Jesus: And it would be true. You find time for the things you really love. You can't fool God. Next! *("Entertainment" exits. Lisa enters without a sign.)*

Lukas: Lisa! Hey, you don't have a sign. What do you represent?

Lisa gestures to indicate that she represents herself.

Lukas: Oh, come on! ...No, wait, I get it! A wife and family is a good thing, but it shouldn't be the ultimate thing! *No other gods before me.* Wow, even family!

Jesus: It's not this way to punish you, Lukas. When you worship God and not these other things, they will stay good things! *(Lisa exits.)*

Lukas: That makes sense.

Jesus: Just one more thing.

Lukas: What?

Jesus: Who's this? *(A crippled old man enters dressed in white with a long white beard.)*

Lukas: Oh, him? He's, ...uh ...*God?*

Jesus: Yes, the god in your mind. What's the second commandment?

Faith and Drama

Lukas: Isn't it the same as the first?

Jesus: It's a little different. *"You shall not make any graven images."* In other words, don't make God into your own image.

Lukas: Oh. Well, I don't *really* believe this is what God looks like!

Jesus: Lukas, you're worried and anxious all the time. In your imagination you've created a god who isn't big enough to handle your problems.

Lukas: Wow, I guess that's true.

Jesus: Is this really the God you find in the Bible?

Lukas: No. I know what you mean! I hate it when people act like they know me but they're not listening to who I say I am!

Jesus: It's even more true for God. But no image at all means you can't have a personal relationship with him. *(Jesus hands Lukas a Bible.)* That's why I came. Find your image of him in here. *(Taps the Bible.)*

Old Man: *(Angrily.)* Listen to who *I* say I am! *(Storms off.)*

Lukas: The god I created is kind of grouchy! *(Pause.)* I'm glad *you're* my God, Jesus!

Jesus: Me, too!

They exit together.

---

*Psalm 16:4

Our Father

Characters
Jude
Caleb

Running time: 2-3 minutes

Setting
Jude sits in a waiting room holding a huge stack of papers. Caleb enters.

Caleb: Hi. What are you doing?

Jude: I'm waiting to see the King, of course!

Caleb: The King? *(Sits next to him.)* What's that you're holding, if you don't mind me asking?

Jude: Records.

Caleb: Records?

Jude: Records, notes, appeals... evidence.

Caleb: Concerning?

Jude: Different things.

Caleb: Like what for instance?

Jude: Well, for one thing I keep a record of everything I do and say—and to a lesser degree, a record of what other people do and say. Everything that's good and everything that's bad; I make a note of it.

Caleb: Why?

Jude: In order to make my case, of course.

Caleb: Make your case?

Jude: Sometimes I ask the King for things and I don't get them.

Caleb: Oh. You think he's punishing you or something?

Jude: What I'm asking for are good things. And I'm a good person, at least I try to be.

Caleb: Sounds more like a business meeting than a personal visit.

Jude: What are you doing here?

Caleb: Oh, I came to see the King too. But when I visit I call him by his other name—Father. He's our Father too, you know.

Jude: I know! And you're coming empty-handed?

Caleb: I always do.

Jude: How long do you expect to have to wait?

Caleb: I'm not waiting.

Jude: What do you mean?

Caleb: I can go in any time. I just stopped to talk to you!

Jude: Really? *(Resentfully.)* Aren't you special!

Caleb: Uh, yes! And so are you! The only difference between you and I is that I know he doesn't stop speaking to me when I fail. And he doesn't owe me anything when I'm good.

Jude: I didn't say he owes me!

Caleb: Then what are doing with all this, brother? *(Grabs the papers and throws them up in the air.)*

Jude: Hey! *(Gathers the papers.)*

Caleb: You still think the way the world thinks. Let me guess, I bet you compare yourself to others a lot and life ends up looking really unfair.

Jude: It is unfair!

Caleb: No wonder you're angry at God.

Jude: That's ridiculous! I never said that! *(Thoughtfully.)* Although it does feel like he's angry with me most of the time.

Caleb: He sacrificed his Son to have a relationship with you. Now he wants you to come to him as his child—that's all.

Jude: But what about being good and doing the right thing?

Caleb: The only way to become good is by loving him for who he is.

Jude: *(Repeats.)* Love him for who he is? *(Thoughtfully.)* After everything he's done for me, I still can't stop thinking of him as a boss that I need to please.

Caleb: Who would you rather he was?

Jude: My Father, of course! If I really believed he loved me that much…

Caleb: He loves you that much and more. So much that he's glad to see you every time, no matter what. Look, put that down.

Jude: Then I'll have no defense.

Caleb: You don't really have one anyway.

Jude hesitates a few moments then puts the pile of papers down.

Jude: I feel so… empty-handed!

Caleb: It's just you now! *(They start to enter, stop.)* Oh, what are you going to ask him for?

Jude: Um… nothing! Today, I'm just glad he's my Father!

They exit.

A Play about Love

Characters
Mary
Nicole
Julie
Anne

Running time: 3 minutes

Setting
Four friends with Bibles and notebooks meeting in a Bible study group.

Julie: My friends, I need to tell you something. I love you! You're all so amazing! None of you are irritating, or embarrassing to be around. You're educated and well-behaved. You even dress well! In short, being with you makes me look good! And that's why I love you so much! *(The women just stare at her.)*

Mary: *(Pause.)* Is that what love is?

Anne: As your friend, that's not exactly what I want to hear.

Julie: It's not what anyone wants to hear! Because I just described *using* you, not loving you.

Nicole: And what does that have to do with asking Amy to leave our study group?

Julie: We can't just love the people who give us something back.

Mary: Look, you know as well as we do, it's not that simple.

Julie: None of us is perfect. That's what we're learning in this Bible study! That we should love people whether we feel like it or not and whether they deserve it or not.

Anne: Yes, that was in last week's lesson! Now, can we get on with this week's lesson?

Mary: Anyway, she's late. Let's start without her. What are we looking at?

Anne: Last week we studied I Corinthians 13, the chapter on love. Let's review.

The group reads from past notes.

Nicole: Love never quits, it doesn't give up on people.

Julie: Because God doesn't give up on us.

Mary: Love is vulnerable, sometimes it means suffering.

Julie: Because people aren't always easy to love.

Anne: Love doesn't keep a record of wrongs.

Julie: Because we're supposed to forgive each other.

Nicole: Love always puts other people first. Love is selfless.

Julie: Because Jesus was selfless, even though he was God!

Mary: I have a feeling Julie is still trying to make a point!

Julie: Well, yeah! We're not being very loving towards Amy.

Nicole: She doesn't even notice! She's too busy gossiping about everyone.

Mary: Let's just be glad she isn't here and continue the study. This week we're looking at John 13, the story of Jesus washing the disciple's feet.

Anne: *(Looks in her study book.)* Okay, it says here that Jesus wanted to show the disciples what love actually looks like, so he got down on his knees and washed their feet.

Nicole: Jesus on his knees washing feet! That's incredible to think about.

Julie: He did it knowing they were going to desert him right when he needed them the most.

Nicole: And knowing that Judas would betray him.

Mary: Think about it. For three years Judas learned all about love but his heart hadn't changed.

Anne: He hadn't become like Jesus at all. It was as if he didn't even know him.

Nicole: Oh, wait! I just got a text from Amy. *(Reads silently.)*

Julie: Well?

Nicole: She's leaving the group. She says she doesn't feel welcome here.

Mary: Oh. *(A few moments of awkward silence.)* I feel terrible.

Anne: Me, too.

Julie: We've been studying about love but we weren't able to love the one we didn't like.

Mary: I'm sorry, but it just seems too hard! I mean, how can we love each other the way Jesus loves us?

Julie: We have to believe it's possible. Then try to do it and believe he'll help us. It's the only way our hearts will change.

Anne: And if our hearts don't change then, like Judas, maybe we don't even really know him.

Nicole: *(Thoughtfully.)* I guess we need to figure out how to wash each other's feet then.

Mary starts gathering her stuff.

Anne: Where are you going?

Mary: I'm going to find Amy and ask her to come back to the group.

Nicole: Wait, I'm coming too.

Anne: Me too. *(As she gathers her stuff.)* It occurs to me that Jesus makes each one of us feel welcome, even though we don't deserve it.

Julie: That's so true. Let's all go!

They exit.

A Play about Joy

Characters
Pete
Pete's Conscience
Joe
Joe's Conscience

Running time: 5-6 minutes

Setting
The Conscience stands behind the Character and represents the Character's thought life. They are the same person and should dress exactly alike.

Pete and Joe are co-workers in an office. Pete sings out loud to himself, <u>Blessed Be Your Name</u>. *Joe is annoyed by this.*

Scene One

Joe's Conscience: Oh, man! He's doing it again. That drives me crazy!

Pete: I can't believe I get to use my skills to work for a Christian publisher. It's like my dream job. *(Continues singing to himself.)*

Joe: Yeah, it's great.

Pete: We're really blessed to even have this job, especially in this economy. *(Continues singing.)*

Joe: Yeah, I know. *(He finally can't stand it anymore.)* I'm sorry, but could you stop doing that?

Pete: What?

Joe: Singing. Out loud.

Pete: Oh! I'm sorry!

Pete's Conscience: I didn't even know I was doing it!

Pete: It was one of the songs I was listening to before I left home and it just got stuck in my head.

Joe: Yeah, I like it too, but... you know.

Pete: Oh yeah, no, how annoying!

Pete's Conscience: *(Sings.)* "You give and take away, You give and take away. Still my heart will choose to say: Lord, blessed be your name."

Joe: *(Pete's Conscience stops singing when Joe speaks.)* I'm thankful to have this job too, but you seem to be this happy all the time. I don't know how you do it.

Pete's Conscience: That's you, Lord, 'cause we both know life is not easy right now.

Pete: I spent a lot of time with the Lord this morning so I guess I can't help it. *(Pause.)* I know that sounds, you know... but I actually mean it.

Joe: No, I know what you mean.

Pete: I start out in the morning praising him and thinking about him and it changes the way I look at everything for the rest of the day.

Joe's Conscience: I barely have time to make it to work on time. But I'm thankful too.

Joe: Yeah, me too. I'm thankful. I guess it's good to think of all the good things we have.

Pete: Yeah, all the good things.

Both men smile as their Consciences say what they're thinking.

Pete's Conscience: God, you are my security.

Joe's Conscience: God, you gave me this job.

Pete's Conscience: God, because you are love I don't have to feel lonely.

Joe's Conscience: God gave me so many friends. *(Pause)* I'm really looking forward to Sarah's party tonight.

Pete's Conscience: God, no matter what happens, I won't lose you. You won't leave me.

Joe's Conscience: In the future I'll have a family of my own.

Pete's Conscience: God, you're Sovereign, my life is in your hands.

Joe's Conscience: God, you'll never let anything too bad ever happen to me.

Pete's Conscience: I love you, God!

Joe's Conscience: Thanks for everything, God!

Joe: You're right. We are blessed!

Pete: Blessed to know him!

Joe: *(Happily.)* Hey, if you want to sing to yourself, I don't mind, really.

Scene Two

Same office. Pete's already sitting at his desk holding a letter. Joe rushes in.

Joe: Oh man, I missed the bus! I always get there with a couple minutes to spare, but today it left early! I hate that! They should stick to the schedule!

Joe's Conscience: *(Complains.)* And of course once you miss the bus then you're twenty minutes late!

Pete: Yeah.

Joe: *(Picks up envelope on his desk.)* What's this? *(Opens it.)*

Joe's Conscience: *(Reads.)* Dear Mr. Lambert we're sorry to inform you that we no longer have the funds to...

Joe: Wait! What? I can't believe it! I lost my job?

Pete: I know, I'm really sorry. We knew it might happen.

Joe: Easy for you to be so calm! Nothing bad ever happens to you!

Pete: Actually, I got the same letter. *(Joe is already absorbed in his own thoughts.)*

Joe's Conscience: Okay, calm down. I've got to think.

Pete's Conscience: *(As Pete stares at the letter.)* Thank you Father, I love you so much.

Joe's Conscience: Why is God doing this to me?

Pete's Conscience: God, even though I can't understand what you're doing right now...

Joe's Conscience: Everything's out of control.

Pete's Conscience: I know you're in control. I rejoice in your wisdom.

Joe's Conscience: If God loves me, how could he let this happen?

Pete's Conscience: I know you love me more than I can imagine.

Joe's Conscience: God, you don't know what it's like!

Pete's Conscience: You took the only real suffering that can take me under.

Joe's Conscience: What's going to happen to me?

Pete's Conscience: I know this is a passing and temporary thing.

Joe's Conscience: I could lose everything!

Pete's Conscience: But it's impossible to lose you.

Pete: *(Takes a deep breath, relieved.)* I guess the only thing to do is to start thinking about what to do next. *(He stands to get a cup of coffee.)*

Joe: *(Slightly sarcastic.)* Yeah, that's all we have to do.

Pete and his Conscience both look at Joe curiously.

Pete's Conscience: Something's not... *true* here.

Pete: I think you have the wrong impression of me. Earlier you said nothing bad ever happens to me, now you're acting like this didn't just happen to me too.

Joe: Nothing ever seems to bother you very much. You must have a bank account somewhere with money in it for emergencies like this.

Pete's Conscience: Ouch!

Pete: *(Sits down again.)* I don't have any savings. In fact, last week I lost my apartment because I couldn't afford it. So now I'm out of a job *and* I have to find a place to live. There's nothing easy about my life right now.

Joe: Oh.

Pete: This isn't good news, believe me. In fact it makes me feel sick to my stomach. But why should I be surprised when bad things happen to me? They happen to everyone! The main thing is I've learned that I don't have to be controlled by my circumstances.

Joe: And how does that work?

Pete: First of all, as a believer you have to *think*. It's not magic.

Joe: Are you telling me it's a choice? If I just choose to be happy I will be?

Pete: Not if you focus on your emotions. But if you focus on what's true, joy will come.

Joe's Conscience: Okay, Father, help me to remember what's true.

Pete: This is how God transforms our hearts and makes us able to handle anything. Don't you want a great heart?

Joe: It wasn't on my list, actually. But I think it's on God's list! *(Smiles weakly.)*

Pete: We can go someplace quiet and pray about this, if you want.

Joe: Sure, thanks! *(Joe and Pete exit.)*

Joe's Conscience: *(To Pete's Conscience as they exit.)* Actually, I'm starting to feel better already!

A Play about Peace

Characters
John
Monique
Beth

Running time: 3 minutes

Setting
Three people stuck in an elevator. John and Monique stand. Beth sits on the floor between them.

John: It's taking longer for them to fix this elevator than I thought.

Monique: What if they're not fixing it? What if they're eating lunch?

Beth: *(Hugs herself with her eyes closed.)* Oh, please don't let that be true!

John: They know we're stuck in here.

Beth: Thank you, Jesus! Thank you for that!

John: It's illogical to think they'll just leave us here! Now that I think about it, it's only been about 15 minutes. We have to give them time.

Beth: Your watch is wrong! I'm pretty sure it's been hours.

Monique: Why is this happening?

John: What do you mean?

Monique: We're at a Christian retreat! Why would God let this happen to us, especially at a Christian retreat! I mean, there's no reason for it.

John: No reason that we know of. This stuff happens. At least we can be at peace about it.

Monique: Peace? I wish! My mind is running in a million different directions.

John: Think of it as the perfect opportunity to focus on all the beautiful things we know are true about God.

Monique: Well, that's a great idea but… How much longer do you think we're going to be stuck in here?

Beth: I'm claustrophobic! Must think of other things…

John: We don't have to be anxious about anything because the Lord is near. Remember?

Monique: But we're missing the worship. That's my favorite part! How am I going to be blessed stuck in this elevator?

John: Jesus gave us *his* peace. You have the kind the *world* gives.

Monique: Meaning?

John: You have the kind that comes and goes.

Beth: Oh, it's gone. Definitely gone.

John: This reminds me – the enemy can't take away our salvation so he does everything he can to destroy our sense of peace.

Monique: I understand that, but it feels like there's nothing I can do about it.

Beth: No, nothing to do. Just try to hold on.

John: We did pray about it…

Monique: Yes. And you said, *And we thank you, no matter how long it takes*!

John: You know, if we didn't have troubles we wouldn't need peace. The idea is to have peace in the eye of the storm.

Beth: Definitely needing some peace right now!

Monique: But it's taking so long! It feels like we're running out of air. I'm sure God didn't mean for us to be in here this long.

John: He obviously does. See, you think you know better than God. No wonder you're full of fear.

Monique: (*Pause*) I know you're right, but I can't help myself. It reminds me of the time I got lost when I was a kid. I was holding my father's hand. For some reason he let go and we got separated. I remember feeling terrified and helpless—like I was never going to get back. This feels the same.

John: Maybe if we all just be still and listen.

Monique: Listen for what? The workmen?

John: No, I mean, just listen. Let the Holy Spirit remind us of what's true so we can have the peace that God gives.

They all wait in silence with their eyes closed. After a few moments...

Monique: *(Eyes still closed.)* I'm meant to hold my Father's hand. I was born to go through life holding his hand.

John: What?

Monique: My heavenly Father …he never lets go of my hand. He's so much bigger than me, so much bigger than this. I'm not pulling away now. I'm so happy to have my hand in his!

John looks at Monique, surprised.

Monique: Thank you, Father. I feel so much better! *(Opens her eyes and looks down at Beth.)* What about you Beth? Are you okay?

Beth: *(Eyes closed.)* I'm Mary sitting at the feet of Jesus. I hear him saying that it's okay. I have the one thing that's necessary and it can't be taken away from me. *(Pause.)* I'm looking up at him! He's smiling at me!

Beth opens her eyes. John and Monique help her up. They hear a voice off stage.

John: Did you hear that? It's the workmen asking if we're okay!

Monique: *(Yells...)* Don't worry, we're fine! *(To John and Beth...)* Hey, anyone want to sing some worship songs while we're waiting?

Monique starts to sing, the others join her as the lights fade.

A Play about Patience

Characters
Susan
Susan's Conscience
Receptionist
Receptionist's Conscience
Jesus

Running time: 3-4 minutes

Setting
A waiting room. There are two chairs downstage where the Receptionist and her Conscience are sitting. Two chairs further upstage. Susan is sitting and her Conscience is standing behind her. There is a rolled up newspaper on the empty chair.

The Conscience represents the thought-life of the character. They are the same person. They should dress exactly alike.

Susan: *(Anxious.)* I've been waiting here for hours!

Susan's Conscience: You're exaggerating! Be patient!

Susan: Yes! Thank you, dear Conscience, for telling me that—for the hundredth time.

Susan's Conscience: You're welcome. That's what a conscience is for.

Susan: Unfortunately, it's not helping. *(Pause.)* That receptionist really doesn't like me!

Susan's Conscience: Okay, now you're being paranoid!

Susan: No, seriously. She's letting people go ahead of me. That's not professional behavior.

Susan's Conscience: It's very possible there's a reason for it. Something going on that you're not aware of.

Susan: Yes, yes …you're probably right.

After a few moments…

Susan: She won't even look at me!

Susan's Conscience: You could just ask her…

Susan: Ask her what? She knows I'm here! *(Susan's Conscience just looks at her.)* I know, I know. *(After a few moments.)* But what if she is being unfair?

Susan's Conscience: What? What would you like to do?

Susan: Honestly, I just feel like lashing out. I'm stressed! I need this job. If I could be rude it would just make me feel so much better.

Susan's Conscience: Okay, let's try it out as a daydream if you think it will help. *(Susan doesn't answer but doesn't stop her.)*

Susan's Conscience picks up the rolled up newspaper someone left on the chair, walks over to the Receptionist's Conscience and hits her over the head with it.

Receptionist's Conscience: Ow! Are you crazy? No civilized person behaves like that! You're a self-absorbed jerk with no self-control whatsoever!

Susan's Conscience: *(Returns to Susan.)* How'd that work for you?

Susan: No, forget it! I look like a lunatic! I'm so ashamed! I can't believe I even had an impulse like that.

Susan's Conscience: I agree! I don't like that image of us at all!

A few moments pass, all is calm. Then...

Susan: She's still ignoring me! I could try a different tactic to let her know how I feel. This time not so obvious! *(Glances at Conscience and nods.)*

Susan's Conscience: A different tactic, a different daydream—well, okay! Here goes...

Susan's Conscience walks over to the Receptionist's Conscience and just stands there.

Receptionist's Conscience: Hello. How are you? *(Susan's Conscience coldly ignores her.)* Uh, can I help you?

Susan's Conscience: I'd like life to be fair, but that's probably asking too much!

Receptionist's Conscience: Excuse me?

Susan's Conscience: I mean, wouldn't it be great if everyone just did their job in a professional, unbiased manner? Wouldn't that make life better for everyone?

Receptionist's Conscience: *(Confused.)* Yes ...I suppose so.

Susan's Conscience: *(Condescendingly.)* I thought we'd agree because you seem like such a *reasonable* person!

Receptionist's Conscience: Oh, uh. Thank you.

Susan's Conscience: *(Smiles insincerely.)* You have a nice day! *(Leaves the Receptionist's Conscience confused and offended.)*

Susan: That was even worse! Please tell me I'm not that person!

Susan's Conscience: Hey, I just represent your thought-life. Don't blame me.

Susan: I don't want to behave this way. I don't even want to think this way! But every minute is starting to feel like an hour!

Jesus enters.

Jesus: I know what you mean.

Susan's Conscience: Oh, it's you, Jesus. You finally got through!

Jesus: I've been trying since you left the house!

Susan: I've been so preoccupied! I've been waiting forever and this receptionist isn't calling my name.

Jesus: Your times are in God's hands—you said you believed that.

Susan: I do believe it!

Jesus: No, I'm sorry to tell you, but you really don't. I know because you've been sitting here grumbling for the last hour. By the way, who do you think you've been grumbling against if God is in control of your schedule?

Susan: Oh… I wasn't thinking of it like that. I know I was being a little impatient.

Jesus: Impatience is you trying to take your life out of God's hands. It's the excuse humans use to commit every other sin.

Susan: Oh, man! This is more serious than I thought. I'm such a jerk!

Jesus: Don't beat yourself up. That's why I'm here, to remind you because I know it's not easy. It is a great opportunity for you to practice trusting me though.

Susan: Oh, Jesus! I was so busy trying to control everything, I wasn't even thinking of you! Thank you for bringing me back to my senses. I love you so much!

Jesus: I love you too. More than you know. From now on, whenever you're waiting on someone, just remember who it is you're really waiting on. *(Exits)*

The receptionist turns and looks at Susan who smiles at her.

Receptionist: Ms Peters? The person in charge of your interview just called. Apparently he had an emergency, that's why he's so late.

Susan: Of course, I understand. Those things happen.

Receptionist: He wonders if you wouldn't mind coming back tomorrow. Same time?

Susan: Yes, I'll come back tomorrow. Thank you.

Receptionist: No, thank *you* for being so gracious! You waited a long time for nothing. And you didn't take it out on me! That's rare. I know because I deal with people all day long, and mostly they're rude and impatient. You're different!

Susan's Conscience: *(Prays.)* Thank you, Jesus. I love you so much!

Susan: *(To receptionist.)* Not really, it's just that I'm in love. When you're in love, a thousand years is like a day!

Exits.

A Play about Goodness

Characters
Jake
Jake's Conscience
John
Jan
Jesus

Running time: 5-6 minutes

Setting
Jake and his Conscience are the same person and should dress exactly alike. Jake sits on a public bench reading a newspaper. His Conscience is standing behind him.

Jake's Conscience: I know you're enjoying your paper but don't you think you should be at work?

Jake: And I know you're my Conscience, but don't you think you could stop making me feel guilty?

Jake's Conscience: I think that's my job.

Jake: Well, I think it's my job to ignore you!

Jake's Conscience: Obviously! Oh great, look who's coming! *(John enters.)*

John: Oh, hi Jake. I was hoping you'd be here. I need to talk to you about something.

Jake's Conscience: Now what?

Jake: Sure, buddy. What's up?

John: I'm sure you've heard that I want to run for president of our Thursday night group?

Jake's Conscience: Which you have no chance of winning!

Jake: So I've heard!

John: Well, here's the thing. There are some people who think I shouldn't be able to run because I've only been a member for a few months. But I don't think that should matter.

Jake's Conscience: Of course you don't.

Jake: Well, if you feel you can do the job then you should be able to run.

John: Exactly! They're saying I wouldn't have the necessary experience.

Jake's Conscience: That's probably true.

Jake: I'm sure that's not true.

John: They might bring up past examples to make a point.

Jake's Conscience: Of course they will.

Jake: That's not fair.

John: There's going to be a discussion about it at the meeting tonight. I could really use the support. Are you going to be there?

Jake: Oh, yeah, without a doubt! I'll be there.

John: Thanks, Jake. I knew I could count on you. See you tonight then. *(Exits.)*

Jake's Conscience: Probably won't now.

Jake: Sure, bye.

Jake continues to read the paper. Jan enters stage left and sits beside him.

Jan: Hi Jake, how are you?

Jake's Conscience: Here we go.

Jake: *(In a very friendly tone.)* I'm great. How are you, Jan? Good to see you!

Jan: Thanks! You too. I saw you sitting here and I was wondering if you were coming to the meeting tonight?

Jake: Uh, yeah. I'll be there.

Jan: Good. Because there's going to be a vote on setting limitations on who can run for leadership positions. It's important, don't you think?

Jake's Conscience: What a control-freak!

Jake: Absolutely. Not just anyone should be able to run.

Jan: I mean, nothing against anyone. It's just a matter of being wise.

Jake: If we're not wise, there'll be problems later on.

Jan: Great. I'm glad you agree.

Jake: Of course.

Jan: See you tonight then! *(Exits.)*

Jake's Conscience: Now I *have* to go to the meeting! Oh well, I'll sit in the back.

The Jesus enters and sits next to Jake. Jake doesn't look up from his paper.

Jake's Conscience: *(To Jake.)* Uh, hello! Sending a message to myself!

Jesus: So what do you really think about the leadership issue?

Jake: *(Without looking up.)* I don't know and I don't really even care.

Jesus: Maybe you should have said that.

Jake's Conscience: Attention self!

Jake: *(Sarcastically.)* Yeah, right!

Jake's Conscience: I'm trying to tell you, it's Jesus!

Jake: *(Jumps up startled.)* Oh! Uh… Yes, you're right, of course!

Jesus: What you say is different than what you think. You're different with different people. Did you know that?

Faith and Drama

Jake: I, uh… I haven't really thought about it. It's just a way of making people happy.

Jesus: It's a way of making *you* happy. You want everyone to like you.

Jake: I guess so.

Jesus: *(Pause.)* It's lying.

Jake: I'm just a people-pleaser, that's all.

Jesus: Brace yourself. I'm going to tell you the truth.

Jake's Conscience: Oh no.

Jesus: You're not taking this seriously enough. It's not just lying, it's laziness, cowardice, hypocrisy, and disobedience.

Jake's Conscience: I knew it was going to be bad!

Jake: That is serious.

Jesus: The opposite of which is being a transparent person. Someone who's sincere and honest with everyone they meet, all the time.

Jake: Getting caught like this does make me feel ashamed of myself.

Jesus: If you're going to be with me you need to be a person of integrity. You've been adopted into God's kingdom, Jake. This kind of hypocrisy isn't possible anymore.

Jake: This is going to take some practice!

Jake's Conscience: A lot of practice!

Jesus: Yes, but this is the only way to become a true child of God. Do you believe me?

Jake: *(Thinks)* Yes, I do. I'll start right away. And I mean that!

Jesus: I know!

Jake: I have a meeting to prepare for. Will you come with me?

Jesus nods and they all leave together.

A Play about Faithfulness

Characters
Beth
Ellen

Setting
Two women are sitting together drinking coffee.

Beth: Ellen, you do this all the time!

Ellen: I just worry that things aren't going to work out.

Beth: But we prayed about this, Ellen. It's in God's hands. Don't you trust him?

Ellen: I try but it's hard. It just seems like he must have bigger things on his mind.

Beth: Bigger than what? He's God! He can probably handle your problems.

Ellen: I know, that's not it. Sometimes I just wonder how long he'll keep putting up with me.

Beth: Oh, so he gave his life for you, but now you're on your own?

Ellen: I have trust issues! I always have. Anyway, thank you for taking care of my little Pajaro this week-end. That helped a lot.

Beth: Oh, it was nothing.

Ellen: I hate to leave him. That little bird is the closest thing I have to a child. I know it sounds crazy, but I love my little Pajaro.

Beth: I know. I got to know him pretty well over the week-end.

Ellen: You did?

Beth: He's not very happy, I have to tell you. I've never met a more anxious bird.

Ellen: Very funny.

Beth: No, I'm serious.

Ellen: Okay, fine. So what's he got to be anxious about?

Beth: He seems to have a deep mistrust of you.

Ellen: Of me? Right! I'm just the one who gives him food and water every day.

Beth: I understand. But every time he needs something he gets nervous. He thinks, "Is this the time she'll forget about me?"

Ellen: That's ridiculous! I love that bird! I named him. I spend hours talking to him. I make sacrifices to make sure he's taken care of.

Beth: *(Shrugs.)* He's afraid you're going to stop caring.

Ellen: Stop caring! How do you stop caring?

Beth: He still worries—that's all I can tell you.

Ellen: I don't understand that. He must think very little of me. I'm a responsible, capable person. More than that, I'm a compassionate person. I'm not some kind of monster!

Beth: You can see why he's insecure though.

Ellen: No, I can't! It really hurts me to think that I've done nothing but love him and in return he doesn't trust me!

Beth: Now you know how God feels! You have faith, Ellen, but you don't think. Do you honestly believe God loves you less than you love that bird?

Ellen: *(Thinking.)* No, I know that's not possible.

Beth: So why do you doubt his faithfulness?

Ellen: I just never thought about it like this before! God wouldn't let me down, any more than I would let Pajaro down. Or anyone else I love.

Beth: Finally! You've come to your senses!

Ellen: I'm the one who needs to learn to be faithful!

Beth: Well, we all do.

Ellen: And you can tell Pajaro he's foolish to worry too. But even if he does, I'll never stop taking care of him!

Beth: Tell him yourself! He's on the balcony. *(As they exit.)* You do know he's not human, right?

Ellen: I know, I know!

A Play about Gentleness

Characters
Soonji
Michael
Kendra
Harold
Joe

Running time: 2-3 minutes

Setting
Friends gossip over coffee.

Kendra: It's just not right! It's shameful, really.

Soonji: He doesn't even try to hide it.

Harold: *(Enters.)* What? What's so shameful?

Michael: The new high school teacher.

Harold: What about him?

They hesitate.

Kendra: He's cheating on his wife!

Harold: What? How do you know that?

Soonji: He flaunts it in public, that's how we know!

Kendra: He's been in my store, so I know for a fact he buys her gifts.

Michael: I saw them in the street together, he was carrying her packages.

Soonji: I've sat beside him in the cafeteria plenty of times. I hear how he speaks to her on the phone.

Michael: All the signs are there, it's so clear what's going on.

Soonji: Carrying on like that in public with a wife and three kids at home!

Kendra: This man clearly doesn't care what people think. How's that for arrogance?

Harold: Now it all makes sense. Yesterday, after school I passed a woman entering the back way. I assumed it was his wife, but then he ran to get her a chair so she could sit down.

Soonji: What kind of a town does he think he's living in?

Joe: *(Who has been quietly listening.)* I think I have a photo of them together.

Kendra: Really?

Joe: *(Pulls out a photo and puts it on the table.)* Is this the woman?

They all stare at it in shocked silence.

Soonji: Why is she in this photo with his kids?

Joe: Because she's his wife. This photo was taken at a church picnic.

After a few awkward moments.

Soonji: I have to pick up my son.

Kendra: I should be getting back to the store.

Michael: Yeah, I have to go to work. See you later!

They exit.

Harold: *(Hands back the photo.)* He's lucky to have a wife like that.

Joe: A wife like what?

Harold: A wife who makes him act like that.

Joe: It's true, she's great! But I know this guy well. He treats everyone with that kind of gentle consideration.

Harold: Well, some people just have a gentle nature.

Joe: No, I knew this guy from before when he was a bully and a jerk!

Harold: Really? What changed?

Joe: Now he tries to be like Christ; the Lion who came as a Lamb.

Harold: Oh, I get it. "Lion" because he's God and God could tear our heads off if he wanted to, but instead he came as a lamb.

Joe: A Lamb who laid down his life for us. I guess we're lucky to have a God like that!

CHRISTMAS

Homeless

Characters
Wise man 1 *(cynical)*
Wise man 2 *(intellectual)*
Wise man 3 *(sincere)*
Man *(traveler)*
Tamar *(woman caught in adultery)*
Abigail *(woman at the well)*
Shepherd
Jesus

Running time: 10-15 minutes

Setup
Imagine the Magi coming back to the scene of the manger after the earthly life of Jesus has run its course. They have followed his life closely and with great interest only to be perplexed by the outcome. The only set piece is a manger downstage center.

Note
A character representing the presence of Christ is onstage throughout the piece. He nonverbally "interacts" with the other characters through his presence, but they do not acknowledge him directly.

Music plays. The three wise men are gathered around with their eyes fixed on the manger where they last saw Christ as a baby. The Christ character listens upstage. A traveler wanders in carrying a huge, oversized burden on his back. They only acknowledge him when he crosses between them and the manger, momentarily obstructing their view. The music fades.

Wise man 2: Hey, get out of the way! I can't see!

Wise man 1: Look out!

Wise man 3: What's wrong with you!

Man: *(Sounding victimized.)* What?

Wise man 1: *(Ignores the Man)* "Where is He who was born King of the Jews?" that's what we said to Herod that day.

Wise man 2: That's right. It was just over thirty-three years ago. We were looking for him so that we could worship him.

Wise man 3: Herod himself had the chief priests and teachers of the law checking the scriptures to find out where this baby, who was Jesus, was to be born. All of Jerusalem was talking about it.

Wise man 2: It was Herod who finally pointed us in this direction!

Wise man 3: And then we followed the star to this place. What an amazing time!

Wise man 1: Yes, remember the trouble Herod went to in order to get rid of that baby? All those innocent children he had slaughtered! Was he really so afraid of a baby who was supposed to be king!

Wise man 2: The prophets pointed to it for so long.

Man: Pointed to what? *(The three men ignore him.)*

Wise man 3: It wasn't mentioned only in the ancient scriptures. Even in our time it was well documented.

Wise man 2: (*Looking through his notes.*) It started with Zechariah being struck dumb in the temple, followed by his wife Elizabeth's miraculous pregnancy, which turned out to be John the Baptist, by the way. Everyone in the region knew about that.

Wise man 1: Followed fast by the birth of you-know-who.

Man: Who?

Wise man 3: Then there was Simeon's proclamation after the baby was brought to the temple.

Wise man 2: Wait, wait a minute! I've got that in my notes! (*The others roll their eyes. He reads from his notes.*) "For my eyes have seen your salvation, which you have prepared in the presence of all people, a light for revelation to the Gentiles and for glory to your people Israel." And there was the prophetess Anna who spoke about him in the same way to anyone who would listen.

Wise man 3: Don't forget about the shepherds of course who heard about it straight from the angels.

Wise man 2: We never met the shepherds.

Wise man 1: What difference does that make?

Wise man 3: (*Reading excitedly.*) "A multitude of heavenly host praising God and saying, 'Glory to God in the highest, And on earth peace among men with whom He is pleased!'"

Man: Really?!

Wise man 2: It had been prophesied for centuries and it happened with a bang, that's for sure.

Wise man 1: *(Moving closer in to the manger.)* Yes, we really thought something was going to come of it at the time. *(Pause.)* What happened?

After a minute of reflection, the discussion resumes.

Wise man 3: Homeless as an adult, I understand.

Man: Homeless?

For the first time the traveler is acknowledged. They stare at him.

Wise man 1: What is that *thing* on your back, and why don't you take it off?

Man: I can't. It seems like I've been carrying it forever. It just grows bigger and bigger. If I leave it on, I feel guilty, but if I take it off, I feel more guilty. The more I try and get rid of it, the heavier it gets. I don't know. I'm worried that in the future—

Wise man 1: *(Interrupts abruptly and sarcastically.)* Heavy?

Man: Very! Who were you talking about?

Wise man 2: The man, Jesus. A king, or so we thought. We thought, possibly even God himself. Listen to this! *(Reads from his notes.)* "All this took place to fulfill what the Lord had said through the prophet: 'The virgin will be with child and will give birth to a son, and they will call him Immanuel'— which means, God with us."

Man: God with us?

They all take a few moments to ponder this.

Wise man 3: But how could it have ended the way it did then? What does it mean?

Wise man 1: And what kind of God would be born in a manger?

Man: Maybe one who knows life is hard.

Wise man 1: (*Ignores the man's remark.*) Or come as a child in the first place?

Wise man 2: It's recorded in the book of Genesis that a descendant of Eve would come to crush the head of Satan.

Wise man 1: And *die*?

Wise man 2: Well, what do you make of this? (*Reads.*) "He forgave us all our sins, having canceled the written code, with its regulations, that was against us and that stood opposed to us; he took it away, nailing it to the cross. Surely he took up our weaknesses and carried our sorrows."

Man: God did that for us?

Wise man 1: So the immortal has become mortal, the unapproachable God has become… *approachable*.

Wise man 2: Why not? It is written, "I am the Lord, the God of all mankind. Is anything too hard for me?"

Wise man 1: Okay, not too hard, but why this way, the way of poverty, suffering, death? Triumph through suffering! Who would have ever thought of it?

Man: Maybe he's trying to teach us something.

Wise man 2: Look, it says here... Just let me find it...

Wise man 1 and 3 look at 2 with annoyance.

Wise man 1: Must you always read from your notes?

Wise man 3: Why can't you just *think*, like we do?

Wise man 2 pouts. A woman approaches, singing.

Wise man 3: What's that?

Wise man 1: What's that? It's a woman singing!

Wise man 2: Look, she's coming this way! Let's observe and see what she does. We may learn something! *(The three wise men move upstage to watch.)*

The woman comes in and kneels at the manger. After a few moments, the MAN speaks.

Man: Did you know him?

Tamar: Yes. He saved my life.

Man: What do you mean? What happened?

Tamar: It happened at a time when I was so unhappy, so unloved. I had to figure out how to live, how to keep going. But the more I tried to make myself feel better, the worse things got. To tell the truth, I didn't care. I did what I had to and that's all there was to it. I wasn't the only one, I knew plenty of people like me.

Then one day something really terrible happened. I don't even know exactly how it started. All of a sudden a mob of men were grabbing me, pulling at me, screaming in my ear, "Adultery! Adultery!" They were dragging me down the street! I knew what it meant but I couldn't let myself think about it. I was terrified. I couldn't understand why they were so filled with hate, such violent hatred toward me. Yet for the man I was with – nothing. Where was he?

Finally they stopped and threw me down on the ground. I couldn't bear to look up; I just knew that I was surrounded by people, a great crowd of people. I heard someone announce to everyone that I had been caught in adultery. I couldn't believe it. I felt like the most sinful person in the world. Then I heard them say something about the Law of Moses and stoning women like me. It was all such a bad dream. They kept repeating the question, "What do you say?" "Well, what do you say?!" I finally realized they were talking to someone. He wasn't answering them. He was also a man, what else would he say? Men forgive men, but not women. He would say *stone her*. I waited for him to say it. I just wanted it to end!

Then I heard a quiet but strong voice saying, "He who is without sin among you, let him be the first to throw a stone at her." My heart stopped. No condemnation? At that moment I realized I had felt condemned my whole life. Then it became so quiet that the only noise was someone crying. It was me.

This man was so different. Surely they won't listen to him I thought. But then I heard the thumping of rocks hitting the ground. Rocks that were meant for me. What's going on? Has the world gone crazy? Was there hope for someone like me? "Woman," I heard the same voice above my head, "where are they? Did no one condemn you?" I slowly lifted my head and looked around; we were alone, there was no one left. I managed to choke out, "No one, Lord." He said, "Neither do I condemn you; go and sin no more."

Jesus saved my life that day – in more ways than one.

Towards the end of Tamar's monologue Abigail enters. Tamar stays on stage. She listens.

Abigail: It was just like any other day; I came to get water by myself like I always did. Just as I started to draw the water from the well I heard a man's voice behind me saying, "Give me a drink." I thought, *oh boy, here we go*. Then I looked at him and saw that he was Jewish! Why was he even speaking to me? According to Jews we're not even human! So I said, "Why are you, a Jew, asking me for a drink?" As soon as he started talking I could tell this was going to be something different. For one thing, he started talking about a gift from God that he could give me. He said if I only knew who he was, I could ask for living water. And he would give it to me!

Living water! See! The Jews have always thought they're better than us! And exactly how was he going to get this water anyway? He had nothing to draw it with and the well was very deep. Who did he think he was? I told him that Jacob himself gave us this well and that Jacob himself drank out it.

He was not impressed by that at all. He just kept talking! He said that if he gave me water I wouldn't be thirsty again. It would be a "well of water springing up to eternal life." Wow! I thought, *well, it would be nice not to have to come all the way down here every day in this heat*! So I said, "Give me some of this water!" Then he said, "Go get your husband, and bring him back here. Why did he ask *that! (Pause)* The man I was living with wasn't my husband. None of my marriages had worked out so...Oh, forget it! This was turning out like everything else in my life! I knew the part about the water was too good to be true! *Okay, just give him an answer, get the water you came for, and go home.*

So I said, "I don't have a husband." Then he said, "That's true" and started telling me personal things about my life! How did he know all that? Then I knew he had to be like a prophet or something. I wanted to believe him but... How could he be a prophet when the Jews were so wrong about basic things? "Why do you Jews say to worship in Jerusalem, when our fathers worshiped right here in this mountain?"

Then he started to talk to me in a way that no one ever had before—like I was a person, and it mattered that I understood. He said the time had come for worshiping in spirit and in truth, that those were the true worshipers, and God was looking for them. God was looking for true worshipers. Why was he telling *me* this? Was he saying that I could be a true worshipper? Was he saying that God was looking for me?

I had never heard anyone talk like this. Could this man be the Messiah? What would he say to that? So I asked him. He said, "I who speak to you am he."

I remember that moment so clearly! I left everything and ran back to the city. I told everyone about him. Then Jesus stayed in our city for two days. People heard and saw for themselves. And afterwards they said that they knew that he was indeed the Savior of the world.

The Savior of the world. Do you know why I was there by myself getting water during the hottest part of the day? Because the other women wouldn't let me join them. They wouldn't even speak to me. But he did. Even now when I think about it, I can hardly believe it. He said, "I who am speaking with you, am he."

Towards the end of Abigail's monologue the Shepherd enters. During his monologue the two women are standing on either side of him.

Shepherd: I'm a shepherd so I know something about sheep. Sometimes they wonder off and get lost. At some point they become so frightened, they just lie down in the bushes shivering from fear. When you find them you have to pick them up and carry them home on your shoulders. I know something about that too.

Tamar: I was lost, who would look for me?

Shepherd: That's the worst part about being lost, knowing that no one is looking for you, no one is missing you. It seemed no one understood my heart. It was like I was crying out but no one heard me. Finally, I turned away from everyone. I didn't feel a part of anything anymore.

Abigail: I had turned away, who would ask for me?

Shepherd: It was clear to me that the good life was for good people—God's favorites. It's easy to love good people with perfect moral records. I thought God was like everyone else. He loved lovable people. I didn't even love myself.

Abigail: I was sick at heart in myself, cut off from hope in the world.

Tamar: When I was alone, I looked for love.

Shepherd: I looked for Jesus. I had heard that when he was born angels told it to shepherds working in the fields. *To shepherds, like me.* So I looked for him. He wasn't hard to find in those days. I was just one in the crowd but it was as if he were speaking right to me. "What do you think?" he said, "If a man has a hundred sheep, and one of them has gone astray, does he not leave the ninety-nine on the mountains and go and search for the one that is lost?" I wanted to shout, "Yes!"

Tamar: I would ask, "Who loves me?"

Shepherd: Was he saying that God loved me? That he was looking for me? The words spoke to my heart. I understood what he was saying, but I could scarcely believe it. He had left the 99 and was looking for *me*! I was being found by a God I hadn't dreamed existed.

Abigail: Christ, you *would* find me.

Shepherd: Then Jesus said, "And if it turns out that he finds it, truly I say to you, he rejoices over it more than over the ninety-nine which have not gone astray." *(Pause)* The idea that God would rejoice over *me*! It made me want to come to him, and I did. And later, when he himself was sacrificed like a lamb, I knew it was so that I would never be lost to him again.

Tamar: You left the 99 who knew you, and looked for me.

Shepherd: Now when one of my sheep goes astray I look for it until I find it. And when I see it alone and shivering in the bushes I pick it up and carry it on my shoulders. And all the way home, I'm thinking of my Lord and remembering how lost I once was. But now, I'm home!

[Dance. Optional] Abigail, Tamar and the Shepherd perform a worship dance. During the dance the Christ character leaves the stage unnoticed. The MAN tries to join in the dance but the burden on his back makes it too difficult. He finally gives up and by the end of the dance he is kneeling over the manger.

[OR no Dance] As Abigail, Tamar and the Shepherd exit, the Wise men move downstage. The Christ character has left the stage unnoticed during the Shepherd's monologue.

The three wise men stop downstage of the manger and say the following lines before exiting. The MAN and the manger are behind them.

Wise man 1: You can't rule men by love. Any king knows that. People understand three things – fear, greed and the promise of security.*

Wise man 2: The evidence doesn't support that in this case.

Wise man 1: The evidence! Why couldn't he just be a king we can understand!

Wise man 3: He's not like us. That's the point.

The three Wise men exit. The MAN is left alone at the manger. Now that the Wise men have left we hear him weeping. He looks up toward heaven.

Man: I think I understand, Lord, I think I understand. Is it too late? Are you still there?

He lowers his head and continues to weep. Music plays. The Christ character enters from stage right, he walks behind the MAN and removes the "burden" from his back and leans it against the side of the manger. Then Christ offers him his hand; the MAN takes it and stands. They hug then exit, the Christ character first. Lights down except for a spotlight on the manger with the burden leaning against it. Music fades out.

---

*Dorothy Sayers, *The Man Who Would Be King*

Joseph's Dream

Characters
Gabriel
Isaiah
Joseph

Running time: 3 minutes

Setting
Gabriel and Isaiah stand above Joseph looking down on him. He is asleep in a chair having a fitful dream.

Gabriel: My name is Gabriel, I'm an angel of the Lord. It's my privilege to deliver messages on behalf of the Lord, God to mortal men. In this case to Joseph, whom you see here.

Isaiah: And my name is Isaiah, I'm a prophet of the Lord. Yes, we're here to give a message to Joseph by entering into his dream.

Gabriel: As you can see, it's more of a nightmare! It all has to do with the birth of Jesus the Messiah.

Isaiah: Joseph was engaged to be married to the young woman, Mary. But he just found out that she's pregnant.

Joseph: *(Startled, jumps to his feet.)* Pregnant! Unbelievable! I've known her family all my life! I never would have guessed this! It turns out Mary is either unfaithful or… or mentally unstable!

Isaiah: Joseph, are you wondering about Mary?

Joseph: What? Who are you? Am I dreaming?

Gabriel: You seem troubled over what to do about the engagement.

Joseph: What she's done is against God's law. I could go public and completely ruin her, but I'm better than that. No, I'll quietly break off the engagement for her sake. It's the right thing to do.

Isaiah: That's generous of you. But like most people, you don't have a clue what God is doing in your life, do you?

Joseph: She'll be disgraced eventually but not because of me.

Gabriel: We have a message for you, Joseph! Don't be afraid to take Mary home as your wife! What is conceived in her is from the Holy Spirit.

Joseph: Conceived by the Holy Spirit?

Isaiah: Yes! Fulfilling this prophecy: "The virgin will conceive and give birth to a son, and they will call him Emmanuel, which means, *God with us*."

Joseph: "God with us"?

Isaiah: It's what the human race has been waiting for! God is coming along side us. He's making it possible for humans to have an intimate, personal relationship with him!

Joseph becomes more anxious.

Gabriel: I told you Joseph, don't be afraid!

Joseph: What? What did you say?

Isaiah: He said, don't be a coward!!

Gabriel: To play your part in God's plan takes courage. No matter how you try to explain it—everyone will judge you, everyone will hate you.

Isaiah: You have to be willing to endure the world's disdain to be a part of God's plan. Mary is willing to suffer the disgrace. Are you?

Joseph: Tell me again what's happening?

Gabriel: Mary will give birth to a son, and you are to give him the name Jesus, because he will save his people from their sins.

Isaiah: Do you accept your part in this adventure?

Joseph: If what you say is true, then of course. I will raise him as my own. I'll give him my name.

Isaiah rolls his eyes and Gabriel shakes his head.

Gabriel: You will not name him. God will name him!

Joseph: What? Every parent has the right to name their child!

Gabriel: Exactly. God, his father, will name him.

Isaiah: This child is God... He will eventually be naming you!

Gabriel: The world needs a Savior, Joseph. And so do you. You think of yourself as a good man but being good is not enough. God wants more than that.

Isaiah: The name "Jesus" means "God saves". Remember what Gabriel just told you; he will save his people from their sins.

Gabriel: Do you believe this message from God, Joseph? Are you willing to let God have his way in your life so that the world may be saved?

Joseph: *(Becoming calm.)* Yes. I think I finally understand. This baby is being born for all of us—including me. *(Repeats.)* This baby is being born for me.

Isaiah: *(Tests him.)* Mary can't escape her disgrace, but you still can...

Joseph: No! Her disgrace will become mine.

Isaiah: Finally!

Gabriel: Okay, it's time.

Gabriel and Isaiah: Joseph, wake up!

Joseph: *(Wakes up.)* Yes! Amazing! It's the most amazing thing. ...I know what I have to do! *(Looks up)* Yes, Lord. I will do as you say. I'm still afraid, but ...I'll obey. I'll take Mary home as my wife. She will give birth to a son and his name will be Jesus, the Savior of the world. ...Let the adventure begin!

Joseph exits.

The Gift

Characters
Aaron
Brian

Running time: 2-3 minutes

Setting
Aaron and Brian are best friends. Aaron enters stage right, Brian left, as if running into each other on the street. They are both carrying bags, which contain the cards and gifts.

Aaron: Hey, Brian! How are you, man?

Brian: Good, good! How's it going for you?

Aaron: Not bad. Hey, I drew your name in the secret Santa draw.

Brian: I drew *your* name! What a coincidence!

Aaron: I got you an amazing gift, you'd better like it.

Brian: Actually, I'm pretty sure the gift I got you is better.

Aaron: What makes you think that?

Brian: Well, for one thing, I did research.

Aaron: Research?

Brian: I asked your family and friends what you like. Even your grandmother and she is really hard to talk to. She couldn't hear me! I had to yell! She was useless anyway.

Aaron: Hey! That's my grandmother!

Brian: No, no. She was great. I just mean she kept saying things like *(in a grandmother voice)*, "Well, he likes chocolate. He likes the color red."

Aaron: What's wrong with that?

Brian: I was trying to find out what you like *best*, not the *every day* things.

Aaron: I did research too. I asked your family *and* at least 300 people who may or may not know you on Face book.

Brian: I shopped in three different neighborhoods!

Aaron: I spent hours on the internet!

Brian: I definitely went over the money limit they gave us.

Aaron: Me too! In fact, I saved up for a year.

Brian: I went without lunch for a year.

Aaron: I walked to school instead of buying a bus card.

Brian: I got a part-time job!

Pause.

Aaron: Actually, I didn't spend that much.

Brian: Me either. But it's still the best gift I could get you.

Aaron: This was the best gift I could get you.

They hand each other the gifts/cards.

Brian: Well, the card is nice but you didn't have to.

Aaron: I didn't get you a card! That'd be expecting a little much, don't you think? Even though you got me one.

Brian: I didn't get you a card either!

Aaron: Then who's this from?

Brian: I don't know!

They put their gifts down (in the manger if there is one on stage) and open their cards.

Aaron: *(Reads.)* Dear Aaron…

Brian: *(Reads.)* Dear Brian…

Aaron: This card was written on behalf of your Father God. I love you more than you can imagine so I've given you the best gift that I could give you.

Brian: *(To Aaron.)* The best gift that *God* can give!

Aaron: What must that look like? *(They continue reading.)*

Brian: I give you my son, Jesus Christ. He is the best that I have to give you.

Aaron: Actually, I'm giving you everything I have because through him I am giving you myself.

Brian: I'm giving this gift to you personally so that you and I can be together for eternity.

Aaron: And so that you can come to me and know me *now*.

Brian: I hope you like it. It's the gift of Peace.

Aaron: Peace between you and me.

Brian: Peace deep within you, and peace with those around you.

Aaron: And of course, this is a gift of Love.

Brian: Giving it to you has cost me everything.

Aaron: But it means that you do not have to live in fear.

Brian: Instead, you can learn my ways and grow in love,

Aaron: in generosity,

Brian: in purity,

Aaron: honor,

Brian: integrity,

Aaron: and holiness.

Brian: In other words, you can live in freedom

Aaron: ...because the time of Grace has come.

Brian: I love you with an unfailing love, my faithfulness towards you stretches to the heavens.

Aaron: And that's why I give you this gift.

Brian: It's the best gift that I could give you.

Aaron: Love, your Father God.

As they put the cards back in the envelope...

Brian: Wow! God gave us *himself*!

Aaron: And it cost him everything! ...What can we give him?

Brian: *(Thinking...)* I think he just wants us!

They start to pick up their gifts, look at each other and decide to leave them. They exit.

The Hope of All the World

Characters
Jairus
Woman
Singer (or recorded)

Running time: 5-6 minutes

The play opens with the first half of the song <u>Mary, Did You Know</u>?

Mary did you know that your baby boy
   would someday walk on water?

Mary did you know that your baby boy
   would save our sons and daughters?

Did you know that your baby boy
   has come to make you new?

This child that you've delivered
   will soon deliver you.

Mary did you know that your baby boy
   will give sight to a blind man?

Mary did you know that your baby boy
   will calm a storm with His hand?

Did you know that your baby boy
> has walked where angels trod?

When you've kissed your little baby
> then you've kissed the face of God.

Music fades. Jairus speaks.

Jairus: I have one child, only one. A daughter, twelve years old. As a leader in the synagogue I have a position of respect and authority. I've always worked hard. I come from a good family. Things have always gone well for me. I was taught if one leads a good life there's nothing to worry about. And if a problem does come up, there's always a solution. I had everything I'd always wanted—I was used to that.

Woman: I'd been sick for so many years I couldn't remember what it felt like to be well or even what it felt like to be human. When you're sick for that long people start to blame you. They wonder what's wrong with you, since you're not getting better you must have done something to deserve it. "God must be trying to teach you something, why aren't you learning it?" Or, "God must be punishing you." And they're not the only ones. I started to think, *God must really hate me. How long is he going to keep punishing me?*

Jairus: Then one day my daughter became sick. Of course I called for the doctors and they did everything they could but nothing helped. I stayed by her side the whole time and watched her get worse. I've never felt so helpless. What was I supposed to do?

Woman: What else could I do? For twelve years I had been to so many doctors, but instead of getting better I just got worse. Finally, all my money was gone and everyone I had ever known had turned their back on me.

Jairus: Then I thought of Jesus of Nazareth. I had seen him heal people with my own eyes.

Woman: I heard there was a man who was healing people, his name was Jesus.

Jairus: I had to find him right away. I would ask him for help before it was too late.

Woman: How could I ask a man like that for help? I was nobody, *and I was unclean*—but I had to try.

Jairus: I made my way through the crowd, it was difficult because everyone was trying to get close to him.

Woman: I was so close to him I could almost touch him. Then he stopped.

Jairus: I finally reached him! *(Kneels.)* My little daughter is dying! Come and lay your hands on her so that she may get well and live!

Woman: A religious leader was kneeling and pleading for something.

Jairus: *(Stands.)* He was coming with me! We might make it in time!

Woman: He was walking away. Wait! If only I could touch his clothing... *(She falls on her knees and reaches out to touch Jesus' robe.)*

Jairus: All of a sudden he stopped. "Who touched me?" he asked! *(Frustrated.)* What? The crowd is crushing him on all sides and he's asking who touched him?

Woman: *(Stands slowly.)* I could feel it! ...I knew it! He healed me, he did it!

Jairus: Unbelievable! Did he forget that my daughter is dying!

Woman: He was asking who touched him. How could he have felt that? How did he know?

Jairus: Finally some woman said it was her. Out of all these people... Why was he talking to her? Didn't he understand what was at stake?

Woman: I was worried he might be angry, or disgusted. But then I heard Him say to me, "Daughter." *(Kneels, weeping.)*

Jairus: *(Falls to his knees.)* Rabbi, please...!

They are both on their knees, one crying from joy, one in despair. Jairus slowly stands.

Jairus: Then I heard someone say, "Your daughter is dead. Why bother the teacher any more?" *(Turns his back to the audience, walks upstage.)*

Woman: *(Stands, crosses to center stage.)* He said my faith had made me well. All I did was come to him. *(Exits stage right.)*

Jairus: *(Turns, faces audience.)* When I arrived at the house people were crying. So it was true, my daughter was dead. He told me to just believe, to just have faith. Then I saw him take her by the hand and I heard him say, "Honey, it's time to get up."

<u>Mary, Did You Know?</u> *song resumes as a little girl runs up the aisle. She and Jairus hug.*

The blind will see, the deaf will hear
   the dead will live again

Montana Lattin

The lame will leap, the dumb will speak
   the praises of the Lamb.

Mary, did you know that your baby boy
   is Lord of all creation?

Mary, did you know that your baby boy
   will one day rule the nations?

Did you know that your baby boy
   was heaven's perfect lamb?

This sleeping child you're holding
   is the great "I AM".

Waiting with a Promise

Characters
Gabriel
Mary
Angel
Elizabeth
Zechariah

Running time: 6-7 minutes

Setting
Music plays. *We see Zechariah, Elizabeth and Mary doing the 'Waiting Dance.' Gabriel is watching them intently, the Angel is silently reading a scroll to himself. As the dance ends and the music fades we hear...*

Angel: *(Reads)* "The promise is based on faith, so that it may be a matter of grace and may be guaranteed for all who share Abraham's faith. Hoping in spite of hopeless circumstances, Abraham believed that he would become the father of many nations."

Ah hah! *(Repeats.)* "Hoping in spite of hopeless circumstances"!

Gabriel: What do mean, *Ah hah*? What's wrong with you?

Angel: You can't fool me Gabriel, something's about to happen. Why else would you be obsessing over these humans?

Gabriel: They are ordinary humans going about their daily lives.

Angel: Yes! But they're also waiting for something. They're "hoping in spite of hopeless circumstances." You can't fool me!

Gabriel: That's right, my friend, you're far too intelligent. Zechariah, Mary, and Elizabeth are waiting... but they're waiting with a promise.

Angel: Ah hah! The promise! I knew it! But the promise was given two thousand years earlier. How can humans wait that long and still be faithful?

Gabriel: Because they're not waiting for something new, they're waiting for something that has already begun, like a seed planted in their hearts that is growing. They're waiting in faith.

Angel: *(Repeats.)* Waiting in faith...

Gabriel: *(Approaches Zechariah who is praying silently.)* Yes, and even when their faith isn't perfect, God is faithful to his promises. *(Speaks to Zechariah.)* Zechariah! Do not be afraid. Your prayer has been heard!

Angel: Oh! It's happening!

Gabriel: *(Continues.)* Your wife Elizabeth will bear you a son, and you are to give him the name John. He will be great in the sight of the Lord.

Angel: Your people have been waiting for this for two thousand years!

Gabriel: *(Motions to the Angel to be quiet. Continues.)* He will bring many people back to the Lord their God. He will make ready a people prepared for the Lord!

Zechariah: How can I believe this? I am an old man and my wife is also old.

Angel: *(Gasps.)* He didn't believe you!

Gabriel: I am Gabriel. I stand in the presence of God and I have been sent to tell you this good news.

Angel: Sometimes I don't know why God bothers!

Zechariah walks downstage. He tries to communicate to the people (the audience) what the angel said, but he is mute.

Angel: Oh, now he can't speak! Is he being punished for not believing you?

Gabriel: No, not punished. But it's unavoidable. When we don't believe God, we become less than what we could be.

Music. Zechariah, Elizabeth and Mary perform the "Waiting Dance" again.

Angel: Something else is going to happen isn't it? I mean, the greatest man in the history of the world, John the Baptist, is about to be born. What else could there be?

Gabriel: Just wait. *(Addresses Mary.)* Mary! *(Music fades out.)* Do not be afraid, the Lord is with you! You have found favor with God. You will be with child and give birth to a son, and you are to give him the name Jesus. He will be great and will be called the Son of the Most High.

Angel: *God* is being born into the world?!!

Gabriel: He will save his people from their sins.

Mary: How is this possible, since I am a virgin?

Gabriel: The Holy Spirit will come upon you and the power of the Most High will overshadow you, and so the holy one will be born.

Mary: I am willing to accept whatever He wants. May everything you have said come true.

Gabriel: The holy one will be born—and he will be called the Son of God. *(Music starts.)* For nothing is impossible with God!

All the characters except Mary turn with their backs to the audience and kneel in worship at this news. Mary walks downstage contemplating the meaning of what's been told her. As the Music fades, Elizabeth stands and speaks to Mary.

Elizabeth: Mary!

Mary: Elizabeth!

Elizabeth: You are blessed among women, and just think of the child you are going to have!

Mary: *(Kneels.)* Elizabeth, then you know!

Elizabeth: *(Makes her stand.)* Who am I that the mother of my Lord should come to me? As soon as I heard the sound of your voice, the baby in my womb leaped for joy!

Mary: Oh, Elizabeth! My soul glorifies the Lord!

Elizabeth: You have believed what the Lord has said. Because of this, you will be truly blessed.

Faith and Drama

Music starts. Mary, Zechariah and Elizabeth perform a choreographed dance. Gabriel and the Angel join the dance towards the end. Dance ends.

Zechariah: He has come so that we might serve him without fear!

All: Without fear!

Mary: *(Prays.)* Lord, thank you for working out your promises. We pray that you would continue to work them out according to your will and not according to our wishes. Amen! *(Mary, Elizabeth and Zechariah exit.)*

Angel: That's strange, why would she pray that? That he work it out according to his will and not according to their wishes?

Gabriel: I think she knows that God's will is not going to be easy, in fact, just the opposite. It's going to be very painful.

Angel: Painful for God, you mean! Speaking of which, why would the Almighty God, the Creator of the universe, agree to come down from heaven? Why would he let himself become so… *vulnerable*?

Gabriel: It's *because* God is so great that he is willing to give up everything. He's doing it for them. He'll do anything to save them.

Angel: Unbelievable! Will humans even be able to understand how amazing this is?

Gabriel: *(Indicates audience.)* See for yourself! Now Christ is also formed in them. See how they love him!

Angel: *(Looks over audience.)* Ah, ha… *(Stops himself, looks at Gabriel.)*

Gabriel: Okay, but this is the *last* time!

Angel: Ah haaaa!

Gabriel signals the angel to follow him and they exit.

Breakable God

Characters
Joshua *(husband/Father)*
Hannah *(wife)*
Daughter *(8 to 12 years old)*
David *(teen-age son)*
Levi
Luka

Running time: 6-7 minutes

Setting
A tea salon in a middle-eastern hotel, which Joshua owns. Joshua and his two friends, Levi and Luka, sit at a table drinking tea. It's obvious they've been talking for hours. They're disheveled and tired-looking. Hannah stands to the side drying tea glasses and cleaning. The daughter sits to the side, fiddling with something.

Levi: It's impossible!

Luka: Absolutely! Impossible!

Joshua: It certainly does seem impossible.

Hannah: That's nice, now you're back where you started!

Joshua: I mean, it's not *impossible*. Nothing is impossible with God.

Hannah: Generous of you to say so.

Levi: No, it's not impossible. But God just wouldn't do it this way.

Luka: No, he wouldn't.

Hannah: So now you have the mind of God! You know what he would and wouldn't do?

Pause. Joshua picks up a book (the scriptures).

Luka: Stop with the reading already. We get it, lots of references to the Messiah coming as a child, a suffering servant, a baby being born right here in Bethlehem – it all fits. *(Sigh)* So many prophecies...

Levi: *(to Joshua)*...all pointing to the baby in your stable as being the Messiah!

Hannah: Well, if it was just you three, I'd wonder. But everyone else is talking about it too.

Levi: Even Herod got involved – which means those foreigners from the east may actually be on their way here even now, looking for a baby king.

Luka: It could be actually happening!

Levi: But why? Why would God become human?

Joshua: Plenty of times in the scriptures he's shown his power through weakness. Maybe he's doing it again!

Luka: Only this time, he's making *Himself* weak. What kind of power is this, I wonder?

Hannah: Why shouldn't God have to experience everything on earth that we have to...if he has the courage and the humility, I mean, seems fair to me.

Levi: Think about what you're saying! 'Everything' would be; poverty, sickness...

Luka: ...hard work, tedium,...

Hannah: *(wryly)*...all the irritations of family life...

Levi: ...pain, humiliation, sorrow, suffering, loss...

Daughter: Maybe he just wants to be near us.

Luka: He'd have to *really* want to be near us.

Daughter: We can't go to him in heaven, so he's coming to us.

Joshua: *(Speaking carefully)* The God of the universe would have to be ... selfless.

Luka: Selfless and ... vulnerable. We don't even do that for each other.

Joshua: If he's risking everything to have a relationship with us then he's showing us that love is worth it. That it's worth becoming weak for the sake of love.

Daughter: *(Pause, then jumps up)* I'm going to see him. *(Mother gives her a look, she responds...)* I haven't been over there once yet today! *(Runs out)*

Levi: Look, I've been religious all my life. I keep the commandments. I tithe. I'm a moral person, I obviously believe in God. So what does this mean? Do I *need* this? What else does he want from me?

Hannah: You're a good person, Levi. But you're not a very *loving* person.

Levi: I admit I'm not good with people. Relationships are hard!

Joshua: His first commandment to us is to love him with all our heart, mind, body and soul. Sounds like a God who wants to be known and loved by us, which fits this situation.

Luka: It's impossible to keep all the commandments, anyway. We can't do it.

Levi: Not that you would know! You don't even try!

Luka: I know, I know. If God wants to punish me, He can do it from a distance! I don't know why he has to come in person! ...What does he want from us?

Joshua: It can't be to give us more information. He could have sent another prophet for that. My daughter might be right. Maybe he came to give us himself.

Levi: God wants to give us *himself*? *(Thinking about the implications)* This is going to require a lot more of me, isn't it?

Joshua: I can't stop thinking about all this. First, that young woman gives birth among all the rumors about wise men seeking to worship a baby king...

Luka: ...Then, shepherds sat right here drinking tea and telling us they came to your shed, Joshua, because angels told them to!!

Joshua: *(Remembering)* "A Savior has been born to you; who is the Christ…" That's what the angels told them. Can it be that this is really coming true! In *my* manger!

Luka: Has the 'unapproachable' become someone we can touch?

Joshua: Has the ideal become real?

Levi: The *ideal*? What do you mean?

Joshua: Think about it! If this is actually happening then God is showing us something about his true nature. He's showing us he's willing to give up everything to get us back. He's risking everything for the sake of love.

Luka: What does that tell us about *our* relationships?

Levi: That keeping the rules is a lot easier!

Joshua: It means that when we lay down the self and do what's contrary to our nature for the sake of love then we are being like God. It may be the meaning of everything.

Joshua's son enters the tea salon. The room immediately becomes very tense. The son starts taking some clothes out of a box and putting them into a bag while he talks.

Son: Still preaching to everyone father? You must love how everyone hangs on your every word!

Mother: David! Stop!

Son: Don't worry. I just came to get the last of my things. You won't have to be embarrassed by me any more.

Luka: I'm the first to admit I'm not perfect, but to disrespect one's father!

Son: Yes. I'm a terrible son and a terrible person! The whole town can't be wrong.

Joshua: Son, stay, I'm asking you to. *(Everyone looks at Joshua in amazement.)*

Luka: What are you saying, Joshua? You deserve respect, not this!

Son: *(Ignoring Luka, speaking to his father...)* What? Why?

Joshua: I don't want you to leave like this, son. Stay.

Levi: You can't mean it, Joshua! What he did was ... it was *unforgivable*! Do you want to lose face in the eyes of the entire town!

Son: Exactly! So why should I stay? So I can live in shame here as your worthless son?

Joshua: What you did was wrong, but I know how it happened. I haven't been treating you like a son. Instead of teaching you and being patient I expected you to be perfect for my sake.

Son: I can't be perfect! I'm sick of trying! Whatever I do, it's not right or good enough, so why bother?

Joshua: I know you've been trying. I was wrong not to acknowledge it.

Son: *(Surprised by his admission.)* Do you think I *want* to embarrass you ... or myself?

Joshua: I've been more concerned about my reputation than about you. Now I just want to be a real father to you, if you'll stay.

Pause. The son suddenly hugs his father and he hugs him back. The mother is quietly crying. After a little while the daughter enters.

Daughter: They're here! The three men from the east who came looking for the baby Jesus, they found him in our shed. Look! They gave me this. *(Shows them a piece of gold.)* They brought lots of gifts. You should see them! They're very rich and their clothes are so beautiful! They look like kings!

Mother: What are they doing?

Daughter: When I left they were kneeling on the ground in front of the baby Jesus. *(Everyone is in disbelief.)* Oh, and his mother told me to invite you all to come see him too, if you want!

Joshua: *(Looking at his son.)* Yes! Let's all go see him together.

The family exits. Levi and Luka hesitate. Levi picks up the scriptures.

Levi: This is a little scary.

Luka: Yes...but I have a feeling, it will be worth it!

They smile at each other and exit.

Behold

Characters
Wise Man
Shepherd
Mary (no lines)

Running time: 3-4 minutes

Setting
The Wise Man (dressed in very rich clothes) and the Shepherd (in poor clothes) are standing upstage left, upstage right. Mary is sitting between them downstage center holding a baby. She has no dialogue. The Wise Man and Shepherd speak to the audience.

Wise Man: I'm a successful guy. Things come pretty easily to me; I come from a good family, had the best education possible, became an astrologer and scientist. I'm well-known in my field. As far as my personal life, I married a woman I adored and we had a beautiful son. So, I was doing as well as anyone can in this life.

Shepherd: From the moment I was born, my fate was sealed. My father was a shepherd and his father before him. I started working in the fields as far back as I can remember. Out in the fields there's not much to do but think. Sometimes I would wonder about God. He obviously set all this up but, beyond that... well he certainly wasn't thinking about me. That's the only thing I was sure of.

Wise Man: I was very sure of myself. I didn't think about God much. The existence of God didn't affect my day to day life so it wasn't important. I was a rational, thinking person who managed my life perfectly well. What was there to think about? Every person is responsible for their own fate.

Shepherd: I knew what I had to do and I just did it. But I was miserable. I used to daydream about being someone else; traveling the world, being important, doing great things... It was a way to escape. But I had to stop. None of it would ever happen. It became painful.

Wise Man: Then the worst happened. My beloved wife died. After that my relationship with my son became really painful. I watched him ruining his life. The more I tried to help, the more he hated me for it. He just wanted me to leave him alone. But my heart was bound up with his. How could I?

Shepherd: I loved one girl and I always assumed we'd be married. But it turned out that was impossible. Being a shepherd wasn't good enough for her family. They knew me, they knew I was a good person, but that didn't matter. That's when I understood my place in this world. Why are some people born with everything and others with nothing?

Wise Man: I began to realize that I couldn't control the things that really mattered.

Shepherd: In the things that mattered most, I was helpless.

Wise Man: If I wasn't in control, was there a god who was?

Shepherd: What kind of a God would make life so miserable?

Wise Man: Does He have a plan?

Shepherd: Does He care about us at all?

Wise Man: I needed peace in my life. Was there a God who could give me that?

Shepherd: If God is in control then I have a problem. I'm not at peace with this God.

Wise Man: When the opportunity came to go on a pilgrimage I was anxious to get away from home for awhile.

Shepherd: Life went on as usual. We were in the fields looking after the sheep. It was a night like any other. The sky was full of stars...

Wise Man: There was an ancient prophecy concerning a star that would come signifying the birth of God in human form. According to these ancient scriptures the time for the star to appear had come!

Shepherd: Suddenly there was a bright light in the sky, it was blinding. It felt, I don't know... *holy*. Then we heard someone from heaven telling us not to be afraid.

Wise Man: As we followed that star I started to think that God did have a plan, and that we were part of it! It was frightening to think about.

Shepherd: We were terrified. Then the angel said that he was bringing good news that would be the cause of great joy for all people. Great joy? What does God have to do with joy?

Wise Man: It was written, "A Savior will be born who is the Messiah, Christ, the Lord. His name is 'Immanuel' which means 'God with us'."

On this line they both move closer to Mary.

Shepherd: The voice continued. It said, "A Savior has been born to you; he is Messiah, Christ the Lord." We ran to the place the angel told us about, and it was just as he said it would be.

Wise Man: We followed the star to a manger. The baby and his mother were there, right in front of our eyes.

Shepherd: We couldn't stop staring at him.

Wise Man: She couldn't take her eyes off him. I recognized the look of love in her face; the love of a mother for her child. From now on her heart would be bound up with his. That's exactly how I felt about my son.

Is this how God looks at us? Could it be? Watching our every move with the obsessive love of a parent? Do we love deeply because the Creator God loves deeply? It was at that moment that I believed. This was 'God with us'. How could he keep away?

Shepherd: Shepherds aren't allowed to testify in a court of law. But God chose us to testify about his birth to the world! Here he was, in this manger, not in a palace. He was one of us. Gazing into his face made me aware of my own bitterness. Of course he came as a Savior because that's what we need. He knows what its like. He's come because he cares. I never dreamed of a God like this.

Mary stands and slowly exits center. The Wise Man and Shepherd watch her leave...

Wise Man: I continued to follow Jesus' life right up until his death, and beyond. Everything in the scriptures concerning him came true. He was the Lamb of God who came to take away the sins of the world.

Shepherd: He was God reaching out and making a way back for all of us.

Wise Man: A way back, a spiritual re-birth that happened the moment I asked Jesus into my heart. Now my heart is bound up with his, never to be separated.

Shepherd: It changed everything.

Wise Man: Nothing is the same.

Shepherd: I sat right next to him in that barn.

Wise Man: I was so close I could reach out and touch him.

Shepherd: But now he's even closer than that. He is born in me.

Wise Man: Why would God come to earth for anything less than this?

Shepherd: The angels were right. God is about joy. He's all about joy!

The two men look at each other for the first time.

Wise Man: Praise the Lord, my brother!

Shepherd: Yes, brother. Praise his Holy name!

They exit together.

EASTER

Peter

Characters
Peter
Woman
Mary
Martha

Running Time: 5-6 minutes

Setting
Music plays. Center stage Peter warms his hands at the fire. The Woman stage left closely watches him. The music fades.

Woman: (*Speaking to the audience.*) I noticed him because I was sitting across the fire from him. I studied his face in the light until I was sure. Then I said, "You were one of those with Jesus, the Nazarene." But he denied it! Said he didn't know what I was talking about! I couldn't believe it! Well, I work for the high priest so I shouldn't have been surprised. Religious people think they're better than the rest of us but they're all just a bunch of hypocrites! All of them!

(*She crosses stage right. Peter turns his back to her.*) It really bothered me because I knew I was right. I had seen him with the Galilean but now he was lying about it. I turned to the others and said, "That man is definitely one of them!" Again he insisted that he definitely was not!

(*Crosses stage left.*) Later someone else in the crowd said that he must be one of them. They could tell by his Galilean accent. Then he really became angry. He shouted...

Peter: (*Angry*) I swear, I don't know him! (*Music plays. Peter begins weeping and eventually exits. Music fades out.*)

Mary and Martha enter the stage left. The Woman exited and appears again stage right.

Martha: Jesus didn't deserve to be abandoned like that. They all just ran away.

Mary: It's too sad to think about.

Woman: Did I hear you say "Jesus"? Are you talking about Jesus the Galilean?

Martha: Yes, if you've heard of him then you must know that he was crucified.

Woman: Yes, I know. But you knew him? Personally, I mean?

Mary: Yes, he was a friend—actually much more than that.

Woman: I heard he did miracles. Did you ever see one?

Martha: A miracle? You could say that!

Mary: Once when our brother, Lazarus, was really sick we sent for Jesus. We knew if he got there in time he could heal him.

Martha: But by the time he finally arrived, our brother had died.

Woman: He died? Oh, I'm sorry to hear that.

Martha: So were we! I told Jesus that if he had come sooner my brother wouldn't have died.

Woman: What'd he say to that?

Martha: I'll never forget it! He said, "*I am the resurrection and the life, Martha!*" (*Thoughtfully repeats.*) I am the resurrection and the life.

Mary: Then he became really upset. He was crying with the rest of us. People said, "See how much he loved him."

Martha: Then he told them to open the tomb. Jesus brought our brother back to us.

Mary: Our brother was alive!

Woman: That was your brother? I remember hearing about that but I didn't believe it! If Jesus knew what he was going to do, why was he crying?

Mary: Because the miracles were just something he did. The most important thing was that he was one of us.

Martha: And now we've heard from Mary Magdalene that he too has risen from the dead! Just like our brother Lazarus!

Mary: Martha, we must find him! All I want is to see him again! *(They exit.)*

Peter appears on a box or behind the pulpit talking to the crowds (the congregation).

Peter: "I know the Lord is always with me. I will not be shaken, for he is right beside me. No wonder my heart is filled with joy and my mouth shouts his praises! My body rests in hope. For you will not leave my soul among the dead or allow your Holy One to rot in the grave. You have shown me the way of life, and you will give me wonderful joy in your presence."

Woman: *(Listens as one of the crowd.)* Is this the same man? What happened?

Peter: Dear friends, think about this! David was looking into the future and predicting the Messiah's resurrection. This prophecy was speaking of Jesus, who has risen from the dead, and we are all witnesses of this. And today he is pouring out his Holy Spirit on us, just as he promised!

Woman: *(Yells at him.)* I heard you deny even knowing him! *Three* times you denied him! *(Peter crosses to the woman.)*

Peter: *(Ashamed.)* I did deny knowing him three times. And when I saw him again after he had risen from the grave, he asked me three times if I loved him. "Do you love me?" "Peter, do you love me?" "Do you love me?" And every time I answered, "Yes, Lord, you *know* that I love you!" And three times he told me to care for his people. "Feed my sheep," he said.

Woman: You! That's unbelievable! How could he trust you? How could he ever forgive you after what you did?

Peter: Because that's why he came. He came to make forgiveness possible. Sometimes I think he chose me *because* I failed him so badly. He needed someone who understood.

Woman: Who understood what?

Peter: That no one is beyond hope—no one.

Music plays. Mary and Martha enter stage right and join with Peter as he exits center aisle. The Woman is left on stage. She thinks a moment then makes a decision.

Woman: Wait! Wait for me! I'm coming with you!

She joins them as the music fades out.

Unexpected Love

Characters
Ethiopian
Philip
Arthritis Woman
Religious Leader
Zacchaeus
Leper
Bleeding Woman

Running time: 6 minutes

Setting
Two stools side-by-side center stage representing the carriage where Philip and the Ethiopian sit. The other characters enter one by one until everyone is on stage for the baptism at the end of the play.

Ethiopian: *(Sits reading a scroll. He stops.)* I'm tired, really tired. *(Stands.)* I've been on the road so long. And for what? I traveled half way around the world to worship in Jerusalem—that's right, to pray in the synagogue. What do you think happened? They wouldn't even let me in! Apparently, I'm considered "unclean" so it's not allowed. I came all this way seeking God just to be turned away and humiliated.

It's ironic actually. I have a very important job in my own country. There I'm treated with respect! I went to a lot of trouble just to be insulted.

What am I doing here? I'm better off than most people I know! Yet here I am ...searching for something more. My friends think I'm crazy! But I can't help it. *(Looks out in front of him.)* In spite of all the success my life is as empty as this desert. I know there has to be something more than this. Where is God? Does he even know I exist? Or is he like this endless, silent desert spread out in front of me? Will I always feel like a stranger in a world that doesn't make sense?

(Picks up the scroll.) There's something here in these ancient scriptures—it seems to have some special meaning but I don't understand it. I must keep searching until I find it... until I find peace.

He sits and reads again from the book. Philip approaches.

Philip: Do you understand what you're reading?

Ethiopian: How can I unless someone explains it to me? Here, sit down.

Philip: *(Takes the book and reads.)* "Who believes what we've heard and seen? Who would have thought God's saving power would look like this?"

Leper: *(Enters stage left, speaks to the audience.)* Who indeed? Who would have believed that the creator of the universe would go so far as to become one of us? Not just a human being but a humble servant named Jesus. Who would have thought God's saving power would look like this?

Philip: *(Continues to read out loud.)* "The servant grew up before God—a scrawny seedling, a sickly plant in a dry land. He was looked down on and passed over, a man who suffered, who knew pain firsthand."

While the characters are speaking, Philip and the Ethiopian continue to discuss silently.

Leper: God didn't spare himself anything when it came to the misery of this life. At the time I met Jesus I had leprosy. As you can imagine, when people saw me they turned away in pity and disgust.

Philip: *(Reads.)* "There was nothing attractive about him, nothing to cause us to take a second look. One look at him and people turned away."

Leper: See! He knows how it feels! He knows what its like to be *me*. I never would have expected God's love to look like this! He didn't have to experience my pain, but he did. It's unbelievable! But I wouldn't want anything less, would you?

Religious Leader: *(Enters stage right)* It wasn't just our illnesses he took on. I was a religious leader in the synagogue; a position of honor and respect. I thought of myself as a good person, a highly moral man. When Jesus of Nazareth came along, my colleagues and I didn't think much of him at all.

Philip: *(Reads...)* "We looked down on him, thought he was scum."

Religious Leader: How could we not look down on him? What did he have of any value? But in the end it was me who came to him for help. He didn't turn me away. He didn't treat me the way I treated him.

Philip: "But the fact is it was *our* pains he carried—*our* disfigurements, all the things wrong with *us*."

Religious Leader: That's just it. He made me see myself the way I really was—inside. My prejudices, my lack of compassion, my pride and selfishness, these were *my* disfigurements, not his.

Philip: "We thought he brought it on himself, that God was punishing him for his own failures. But it was our sins that did that to him, that ripped and tore and crushed him—*our sins!*"

Arthritis Woman: I wasn't looking for him, I didn't ask him for help! I had suffered from arthritis for eighteen years. I had long given up on anything changing. He noticed me in the synagogue and called me over. He laid his hands on me and said, "Woman, be free!" And I was! I was able to stand up straight for the first time in eighteen years. Not only that, but when the religious leaders complained about my being healed on the Sabbath, he came to my defense. He called me a *daughter of Abraham* and told them they were the ones who were the hypocrites! What was this? I always believed in God but I didn't expect him to come and find me. I didn't expect him to love me like this!

Philip: "He took the punishment, and that made us whole. Through his bruises we get healed."

Bleeding Woman: I was desperate! I'd spent all my money on doctors but my disease was getting worse. I thought, *if I could find this man, Jesus, I could be healed.* He was my last hope. I did find him and when I was finally able to get close to him, I reached out and touched the hem of his clothes. I could feel the disease leave my body! For the first time in twelve years I felt like a human being! He said he felt the power go out of him. It was as if he was trading places with me. Later I understood that he actually *was* taking my place—and it cost him his life.

Zacchaeus: It never occurred to me that God would love me. Here I was, a tax collector who only thought about myself. I loved money and I was willing to cheat people to get it. But then one day I went to see Jesus for myself, but of course I couldn't get near because of the crowd. The best I could do was climb a tree and hope for a glimpse of him. But then *he* saw *me* and called me to come down. He called my name in front of everyone! Then he came to my house for a meal!

Before that day I don't think I'd ever done one unselfish thing and he knew it. He knew who I was and he still called me by name.

Philip: *(Stands, steps forward, reading.)* "We're all like sheep who've wandered off and gotten lost. We've all done our own thing, gone our own way. And God has piled all our sins, everything we've done wrong, on him, *on him*."

Ethiopian: *(Takes scroll from Philip and reads.)* "Like a lamb taken to be slaughtered and like a sheep being sheared, he took it all in silence. Justice miscarried, and he was led off—and did anyone really know what was happening? Though he'd never hurt a soul or said one word that wasn't true." I'm beginning to understand. He was the only one who was innocent. He didn't have to die but he died for us—the Lamb of God who was sacrificed for us, once and for all. *(He hands the scroll to the Religious Leader. Sound effect of a running river plays.)* Who would have thought God's saving power would look like this?

The Ethiopian steps forward to be baptized by Philip surrounded by the other characters. The water sound effects fade out, and music plays. Philip silently prays over the Ethiopian. Two of the actors put a white robe on him. All exit as the music fades.

Jesus' Dream

Characters
Pilate
Modern Man (*Wears suit and tie*)
Christ
Mary Magdalene
Angel

                                        Running time: 5-6 minutes

We see Christ center stage. We hear the following lines, which have been pre-recorded with background music, a thunder sound effect at the end. It is as if he is dreaming, or reminiscing during the lines. He is startled at the sound of the thunder.

Christ: 1: *(The lines overlap)* My God, my God, why have you forsaken me? Why are you so far from saving me, so far from the words of my groaning?

2: Scorned by men and despised by the people, I am a worm and no man.

1: All who see me mock me; they hurl insults, they curl their lips and wag their heads, saying;

2: "He trusts in the Lord, let the Lord rescue him. Let him deliver him, since he delights in him."

1: There is no one to help

2: I am poured out like water and my bones are out of joint

1: My heart has turned to wax, it has melted away within me.

2: Dogs have surrounded me, a band of evil men has encircled me, they have pierced my hands and my feet.

1: People stare and gloat over me. They divide my garments among them and cast lots for my clothing.

2: Be not far off! 1: Rescue me! 2: Deliver me! 1: Save me! *(Psalm 22)*

During the last four lines, Pilate (stage right) and Man (stage left) stand and turn towards audience (it works well if they have boxes to stand on). Jesus remains in the center, listening to the two men as they talk to the audience.

Pilate: The path of least resistance has always worked well for me.

Man: The path of least resistance has always worked well for me. I try to get along with everyone, my job depends on it.

Pilate: I told those religious fanatics to take him and judge him by their own laws. Why involve me? I don't want to deal with it. But they're using me. They need him put to death.

Man: Sure, I'm a Christian but it's not that easy in the real world. Sometimes it's hard to do the right thing. Even though I'm in a position of authority, I still have to get along with people.

Pilate: *(Arrogant)* I'm a man of authority. That's why the Jews have brought me this man, Jesus. Now they're saying he's claiming to be king. Sounds like sedition! I suppose I should look into it.

Man: I should look into it. They're accusing a co-worker of stealing. I know this man; he's not well liked in the office because he's different, but he hardly seems like a thief. I don't have a good feeling about this.

Pilate: *(Insecure)* That didn't go well. I started out with the wrong question; "Are you king of the Jews?" Did *I* order him brought in? That's what *they* told me! I don't know! Then I lost my temper. That really didn't go well at all.

Man: *(Insecure)* Proof! Of course I don't have any proof! No one has any proof or they would have brought it forward. But I still have to act on it, everyone's expecting me to. He must understand that!

Pilate: *(Laughing)* Sometimes I enjoy my job. So he starts talking about this other kingdom, a heavenly kingdom. So I said, "So, you *are* a king!" That was a good moment. It was priceless.

Man: *(Confident)* He's lucky I'm a fair man. I'm getting a lot of pressure to fire him just because they're all saying he did it. But I don't think he did. I just have to convince them to drop it.

Pilate: *(Worried)* This man is innocent. I would say he's crazy but when I speak to him I get the feeling he's the one in control. He speaks with such authority. I keep telling them I find no guilt in him but they won't listen. This isn't good.

Man: *(Worried.)* This man has integrity. I know he's innocent! But they won't accept anything less than his being let go. Why do they hate him so much?

Pilate and Man: *(simultaneously)* The only way out of this is to do the right thing.

(The following is frantic.)

Pilate: It's the Passover, I'll offer to let him go.

Man: I'll issue a warning. It will be on his work record but at least he'll keep his job.

Pilate: I'll have him whipped, surely that will be enough.

Man: His reputation is already ruined. Isn't that enough?

Pilate: I'll humiliate him. I'll have him dressed like a king and paraded in front of everyone.

Man: Oh great, now they're threatening to go over my head!

Pilate: "*No friend of Caesars*"! Now they're bringing up Caesar!

Pilate and Man: *(simultaneously)* What do you want from me? *(Pause. They scream...)* Take him!

Christ exits. Silence except for the sound of a woman crying.

Pilate: *(Collects himself)* Oh well, one innocent man crucified. *(Looking at the man.)* No one will remember. *(Exits)*

Man: *(Sits on box, defeated, looks up.)* Jesus, what was I suppose to do? I could have lost everything. *(Remains seated, with his head in his hands.)*

The woman, still crying, enters the stage. The angel enters stage left.

Angel: Woman, why are you crying?

Mary Magdalene: They took my Master and I don't know where they've laid him.

Christ: *(Appears from stage left.)* Woman, why are you crying? Who are you looking for?

Mary: Mister, if you took him, tell me where you put him so I can care for him.

Christ: *(Takes a step towards her.)* Mary.

Mary: (*Recognizing him, she runs and kneels before him. She grabs his arm.)* Rabboni!

Angel: *(Comforts her.)* Don't cry, Mary. See! He has become your salvation. He has done it. It is finished!

Christ: *(To Mary...)* Don't hold on to me, Mary. I need to return to the Father. I'm returning to my Father and *your* Father, to my God, and *your* God. Go! Spread the news!

Music *is heard as the angel helps Mary up and they exit.*

Jesus walks up to the Man, still sitting on the box, and offers him His hand. He takes it. They hug and then exit together.

Water and Wind

Characters
Nicodemus
Joseph of Arimathea

Running time: 3-4 minutes

Setting
Written for a Candlelight service. This play takes place inside the tomb, after the crucifixion. The stage area is dimly lit. A "body" wrapped in white clothe lays upstage on a bench (not on the floor) and is lit from offstage. There are two (safe) candles lit on the set. Both characters are overcome with grief.

Nicodemus: *(Walks downstage, exhausted.)* We made it, Joseph! The day of Preparation is almost over and we finished in time! It was God's providence that this tomb was nearby.

Joseph: Yes, God provided. At least now he won't be buried as a criminal. I couldn't have done it without you, Nicodemus.

Nicodemus: While you were negotiating with Pilate I had time to buy everything.

Joseph: Yes, it all worked out.

After a few moments sitting in silence.

Nicodemus: I guess... now we go home.

Joseph: Yes. Well, anyway ...I feel sick.

Nicodemus: I know. If we leave, then what? Is it over?

Joseph: No... I mean, how can it be?

Nicodemus: His teachings, who he was—that doesn't just go away. "The kingdom of God is among us," he said. I believe we saw it.

Joseph: I waited for the Kingdom my entire life and when it came, I did everything wrong.

Nicodemus: It wasn't what we were expecting, Joseph.

Joseph: No. But I think we knew he was speaking God's words from the beginning.

Nicodemus: At the time it felt like there was too much to lose.

Joseph: Even the temple guards couldn't bring themselves to arrest him. Do you remember? They told the Council that they had never heard anyone speak the way he did.

Nicodemus: I remember it well. That was the first time I found the courage to speak up in his defense. But they scoffed at me and that's all it took. I didn't try again.

Joseph: Fear is a powerful thing.

Nicodemus: You asked Pilot for his body, Joseph. That took a lot of courage.

Joseph: Asking for his life would have been better.

They both fall silent again. Nicodemus gets up and looks out the entrance of the tomb (downstage left).

Nicodemus: *(Yells.)* What do you want?

Joseph: *(After a moment.)* Is she still out there?

Nicodemus: I'm sure that's her back in the trees. She probably just wanted to see where we were taking him.

Joseph: Poor woman, faithful to the end. Speaking of being faithful, where are the others?

Nicodemus: *(Still looking out the entrance.)* A typical follower of his. Look at her. A poor, unclean woman with a history of mental illness—a prostitute!

Joseph: Yet she showed courage when we didn't.

Nicodemus: Yes, yes! I'm sure people will be talking about her a thousand years from now.

Joseph: If they are, they'll also be talking about us. How we loved human praise so much more than the Son of God. If only we could wipe the slate clean and start over.

Nicodemus: *(Pause.)* That's right. *(Thoughtfully.)* It's not just for her.

Joseph: What?

Nicodemus: The new birth. It's not just for her. That's what Jesus was trying to tell me that night I went to see him.

Joseph: New birth? What are you talking about?

Nicodemus: *(Sits)* I remember what he said to me that night in the garden about water and the Spirit. We must be born again; a supernatural spiritual birth that comes from heaven, mysterious like the wind. He said it over and over. Without this second birth it is impossible to enter the kingdom of heaven.

Joseph: Born again from heaven… is it possible? It sounds too good to be true. What else did he say?

Nicodemus: He said he would be lifted up, just like Moses lifted up the snake in the wilderness. Those who were sick and dying were healed just by looking at it. Remember?

Joseph: *(Stands.)* Yes. Something did happen to me when I looked up at him on that cross today. I saw myself as I really am. I saw someone who needed to be healed. Then I heard his voice asking God to forgive us. To forgive *me*.

Nicodemus: I know. Everything I used to think was important just fell away. Something new has begun. I feel it. …Now I know where she gets her courage from.

Joseph: Yes. From love!

Nicodemus: Only love could make a new birth possible.

After a few moments…

Nicodemus: Joseph, we don't need to stay in this tomb.

Joseph: No, I don't think we do. That's the point. We don't have to stay here at all. *(Gathers belongings.)* Okay... Let's try and find that woman and make sure she gets home safely.

Nicodemus: Yes—that is, if she doesn't mind being seen with us! Take the candle and let's go.

They exit the stage with the lit candles. A woman dressed as Mary Magdalene joins them with a candle and the three of them begin lighting the candles of the congregation who then exit quietly.

Sacrifice

Characters
Mary Magdalene
Zacchaeus
Pharisee
Observer
Voice of Jesus

Running time: 5 minutes

Stetting
The voice of Jesus can be recorded or read offstage over a microphone. The actors begin by kneeling/standing with their backs to the congregation facing a (life-size) replica of a cross. One by one they move from the cross to center stage to do their monologues, then to stage left.

Recording 1: *My God my God why have you forsaken me: Why are you so far from helping me and from the words of my groaning? My God I cry to you by day but you do not answer: and by night also I find no relief.*

Music fades as Mary Magdalene moves center stage.

Mary Magdalene: There was no relief from the loneliness and isolation I felt. I couldn't go out during the day unless I wanted to hear, "Adulterer!" "Prostitute!" and other names. I was called mad, evil, possessed. I probably was all of those things at one time or another. Let me tell you, when you sink that low in life, you're alone. No one cared enough or was brave enough to try and help me—just the opposite. When I wasn't being ridiculed or physically abused, I was being ignored. I don't know what was worse. I'm sure everyone thought, *There's no hope for her, what's the use?* They were right, it would take a miracle.

Then one day there he was—Jesus. Some said he was the Son of God. My impression of God was that he only cared about the moral ones, the good people, the ones who got it right. He wouldn't look twice at me. But he did. More than that, he looked right at me. He looked past my pain and brokenness and saw what was left of *me*. I was shocked when he didn't judge me. He didn't turn away in pity or disgust. And most of all, he didn't ignore me—just the opposite. He had come to find me.

(Looks at the cross.) Then it happened to him—the lies, the ridicule, the accusations and torture. *(To the audience.)* When I saw him on that cross, I knew it was for people like me.

Recording 2: *But as for me I am a worm and no man: the scorn of men and despised by the people. Everyone who sees me mocks me: They sneer and shake their heads, saying, "Is this the one who relies on the Lord? Then let the Lord save him. If the Lord loves him so much, let the Lord rescue him.*

Music fades as Mary Magdalene moves stage left, Zacchaeus moves to center stage.

Zacchaeus: I had no right to even call myself a man. I was hated by everyone, and no wonder. I loved money and I was willing to cheat people to get it, even my own people! I didn't care! It was so easy to rationalize it all. I had to survive didn't I? And if other people were left with nothing, that was fate, not me. Money was how I measured everything, even my own worth.

Faith and Drama

But everything changed when Jesus saw me and called out my name. He announced in front of everyone that he was coming to my house for supper. He was going to be a guest in my house! My enemies were just as surprised as I was!

Until that day I don't think I'd ever done one unselfish thing—and Jesus knew that. But he still treated me as if I had value. It made me want to *be* a person of value. In fact, his love changed the way I saw everything.

(Looks at the cross.) When I saw him on that cross I thought, *He's getting the punishment I deserve.*

Recording 3: *Like roaring lions attacking their prey they come at me with open mouths. My life is poured out like water and all my bones are out of joint. My heart is like wax melting within me. My strength has dried up, my tongue sticks to the roof of my mouth.*

Music fades as Zacchaeus moves to stage right, the Pharisee moves to center stage.

Pharisee: I wanted to tear him to pieces! Every time I heard news of him or heard him speak, hatred and indignation welled up in the pit of my stomach. I was a religious leader and he was just a poor, uneducated... nobody! How dare he act like he was better than we were, we who had been called by God! Who had spent our lives serving God!

The people looked up to me. When it came to the most important questions concerning life, I had the answers. I knew who God was and what he expected from us. When that was challenged by Jesus and his teachings I was furious. Can you blame me? I knew then that I had to gather enough evidence to accuse him, and then destroy him.

So I watched and listened. I didn't even recognize the God Jesus was talking about! The God I thought I knew was angry and hard to please. But Jesus talked about God as a Father who was reaching out to us like lost children. A God of love, not condemnation. I started to believe it was true because Jesus himself was, well, everything I wanted to be but wasn't. He had integrity. No one spoke the way he did. I started to see myself as I really was and I began to repent. And for the first time in my life, I stopped feeling like an imposter.

By the time Jesus was arrested I had completely changed my mind about him. *(Looks at the cross)* His death was more than I could bear. When I saw him on that cross, I knew it was for people like me.

Recording 4: *My enemies surround me like a pack of dogs; they are closing in on me. They have pierced my hands and feet. I can count every bone in my body. My enemies stare at me and gloat. They divide my clothes among themselves and throw dice for my garments.*

Music fades as the Pharisee moves stage right, the Observer moves to center stage.

Observer: He didn't have much to begin with. Jesus traveled around the region with his disciples preaching and healing people. He didn't even have a home.

One day he was invited to eat at the home of a friend of mine. As usual there were a lot of people crowding the courtyard, getting as close as they could. Then something remarkable happened. A woman pushed her way in. She was crying and she kneeled down in front of Jesus. Her tears were running down his feet! We were shocked when she took her hair down and was drying his feet with her hair! But that's not all—she kept kissing his feet and putting perfume on them! We just watched in dumb amazement.

I admit the whole thing made me very uncomfortable. I don't know if I was more embarrassed for her or for Jesus. This was a shocking display of emotion and, well, inappropriate behavior. It was nothing short of a public spectacle. What made it even worse was that this woman had a bad reputation, she was a sinner. I couldn't figure out why he didn't stop her. Instead, he defended her! He explained that she knew that her sins, which were great, had been forgiven. So her love was also great.

I understood this later when out of desperation I approached Jesus for help. He had plenty of reasons to turn me away. But he didn't. He didn't even use the opportunity to accuse and judge me—like I had judged her. In short, he didn't treat me the way I treated other people. I experienced grace for the first time in my life.

I often thought of that woman and how her display of love embarrassed us. *(Looks at cross)* But when I saw him on that cross, I thought—*No, she's the only one who did the right thing that day.* *(Joins the others stage left.)*

Mary Magdalene: The fact is, it was *our* pains he carried—*our* disfigurements, all the things wrong with us.

Zacchaeus: By taking our punishment, he made us completely well. The punishment that brought us peace was on him, and by his wounds we are healed.

Pharisee: And now, because of his sacrifice, we are reconciled to God.

Observer: How great a love is this?

READINGS

The Sower

Matthew 13:1-9

Four Readers

Reader 1: Behold, what country does this love come from?

Reader 3: God's kingdom on earth

Reader 4: Healing every alienation

Reader 2: Every brokenness

Reader 3: Social

Reader 4: Economical

Reader 1: Racial

Reader 3: Emotional

Reader 2: Physical

Reader 4: Psychological

Reader 1: Spiritual.

Reader 3: When you enter this place

Reader 2: When the power of God's kingdom enters you

Reader 4: Every area of your life begins to heal

Reader 1: This kingdom of love comes by hearing

Reader 3: So be careful how you listen

Reader 2: Kingdoms on earth are established by

Reader 4: Violence, wars

Reader 1: Force and bloodshed

Reader 3: But God's Kingdom comes gently

Reader 2: Like a seed that is planted and grows

Reader 1: It comes by hearing

Reader 4: So be careful how you listen

Reader 2: It's easy to reject, and it's easy to miss

Reader 3: It starts out as a crazy message

Reader 1: Vulnerable and weak

Reader 2: And not of this world

Reader 4: God came to serve

Reader 1: He came to conquer

Reader 3: By losing everything

Reader 4: Being tortured

Reader 2: And killed

Reader 3: His death

Reader 1: Was the death of all our guilt

Reader 2: And the beginning of life

Reader 3: His life for ours

All: Behold, what country does this love come from?

Reader 4: A heavenly country. And now...

Reader 2: It is in your midst

Reader 3: It comes to you by hearing

Reader 1: So be careful how you listen

Reader 4: It's easy to reject

Reader 2: In this kingdom, the way up is down

Reader 3: The way to find yourself is to lose yourself

Reader 1: The way to power is to become humble

Reader 2: The way to be rich is to give your money away

Reader 4: The way to grow and be transformed

Reader 3: Is to endure pain and suffering

Reader 2: And learn dependence.

Reader 1: This kingdom transforms by love, not by force

Reader 3: It creates loving obedience

Reader 4: Children

Reader 2: Instead of slaves

Reader 4: Eventually this kingdom changes everything

Reader 2: So be careful how you listen

Reader 1: It's easy to reject, and it's easy to miss

Reader 3: A farmer goes out to sow his seed. As he is scattering the seed, some falls along the path, and the birds come and eat it up. He who has ears to hear, let him hear.

Reader 4: Some listen with the mind only

Reader 3: At church,

Reader 2: Retreats

Reader 4: Camps

Reader 3: Youth groups

Reader 1: They hear with their ears

Reader 2: But not with their hearts

Reader 4: It doesn't change the way they see the world

Reader 3: It doesn't change them

Reader 1: So be careful how you listen

Reader 2: It's easy to miss

Reader 3: Some of the seed falls on rocky places, where it does not have much soil. It springs up quickly, because the soil is shallow. But when the sun comes up, the plants are scorched. They wither because they have no root. He who has ears to hear, let him hear.

Reader 4: Some listen with a shallow heart

Reader 1: At first they get very excited

Reader 3: Very emotional

Reader 2: They say, "Christ has changed my life"

Reader 4: But as soon as troubles come into their life

Reader 3: They turn their back on God and say

Reader 1: "What's the use of knowing Jesus if I lose things

Reader 2: If I suffer

Reader 4: If I can't get what I want?"

Reader 1: They worshipped with joy

Reader 3: Until they couldn't get what they really worshipped

Reader 4: So be careful how you listen

Reader 3: Other seed falls among thorns, which grow up and choke the plants. He who has ears to hear, let him hear.

Reader 1: Some listen with a divided heart

Reader 2: The Word of God is personal and it has taken root

Reader 1: But the worries of this life

Reader 4: And the deceitfulness of wealth

Reader 2: Choke it

Reader 3: These believers are always anxious

Reader 1: They can't go back, they know too much

Reader 4: But they can't go forward. Faith

Reader 2: But no fruit

Reader 3: No change

Reader 4: They're miserable

Reader 1: Because they have a divided heart

Reader 2: So be careful how you listen

Reader 4: It's easy to be divided

Reader 3: Still other seed falls on the good soil, where it produces a crop—a hundred, sixty or thirty times what is sown.

Reader 1: These are the ones who hear and understand

Reader 2: They are in the kingdom

Reader 3: —and the kingdom is in them

Reader 4: Eventually, it will change everything

Reader 1: So he who has ears to hear, let him hear

Reader 3: And be careful how you listen!

Reader 2: The kingdom of God is not coming

Reader 4: With signs that you can see

Reader 3: Nor will people say

Reader 1: 'Here it is!' or 'There it is!'

Reader 2: Because the kingdom of God is within you

All: It comes as Love

Reader 4: And how it grows

Reader 1: Depends on how you listen

Lazarus and the Rich Man

Luke 16:19-31; Psalm 73; Psalm 91; Amos 6:4-7

Readers
Jesus
Lazarus
Abraham
The Rich man

Setting
Jesus and Abraham stand on a higher level looking down on Lazarus and the Rich Man. Lazarus is stage right, the Rich Man is stage left.

Jesus: My name is Jesus. This is Abraham, whom I'm sure you've heard of. We want to introduce you to a couple of people who live on earth; one is Lazarus, a poor, homeless man, and the other is a very rich man.

Abraham: The rich man dresses like a king every day. In fact, he lives his whole life in luxury!

Rich Man: So true! Look at my clothes! I spend my days lounging on beautiful ivory couches, eating the meat of tender lambs and drinking wine by the bowlful!

Faith and Drama

Abraham: Lazarus lies at the rich man's gate, starving and sick. He begs for leftover food that's thrown in the garbage. As he lays there hoping for scraps, the dogs come and lick his open sores.

Lazarus: Look at me! My life is draining away. I used to have hope, but now all I do is survive. It's hard not to be bitter about everything I've lost.

Rich Man: Well, I have no regrets! Whatever I have, I earned. No one gave it to me and no one helped me! Whereas this wretched man lies at my gate waiting for a hand out!

Abraham: *(To Lazarus)* Don't put your confidence in powerful people, Lazarus. There's no help for you there. But remember, when they breathe their last they return to the earth and all their plans die with them.

[Note: This section is fast and intense.]

Lazarus: *(Stands)* I admit, there are times when I envy the proud. I watch them prosper despite their wickedness. The rich seem to live without pain or suffering. They have total security.

Rich Man: Why shouldn't I feel secure? I push away every thought of coming disaster. The nation may have its problems, but what does that have to do with me?

Lazarus: *(Complains)* Their bodies are healthy and strong. *They* don't have troubles like other people! They're not plagued with problems like everyone else!

Rich Man: It's true, I know how to enjoy myself. I sing songs to the harp. I make up the words myself, just like David did!

Lazarus: (*Bitter*) They wear pride like jewelry and clothe themselves with cruelty. The rich have everything their hearts desire!

Rich Man: It's fate! (*Shrugs*) What can I do?

Lazarus: My heart is bitter. I'm torn up inside! I ...I'm like an animal! (*Pause. The pace changes. He sits.*) But I know this – the Lord is faithful. His love never ends! I believe this. I know it's true.

Rich Man: What are you mumbling about Lazarus? Here's some change. (*Throws coins at him*) Now, be quiet! Your suffering has made you mad!

Abraham: (*Urgently*) Hold tight to the eternal life to which God has called you, Lazarus. You belong to the Lord. He holds you in his hand and is leading you to a glorious destiny.

Lazarus: Yes! (*Prays*) Lord, who do I have in heaven but you? I desire you more than anything on earth. My health may fail, and my spirit may grow weak, but God remains the strength of my heart; he is mine forever.

Rich Man: Lazarus, you amaze me! Are you still lying at my gate? You always look like you're on death's door, but you never die! As for me, let me get to my dinner!

Lazarus: As for me, how good it is to be near God! I have made the Sovereign Lord my shelter and I will tell everyone about the wonderful things he does.

Abraham: The Lord your God has said, "I will rescue those who love me. I will protect those who trust in my name…"

Jesus: "...When they call on me, I will answer; I will be with them in trouble. I will rescue and honor them. I will reward them with life and give them my salvation."

Lazarus: *(Stands)* Yes, I remember! His mercies are new each morning. The Lord is my inheritance; therefore, all my hope is in him!

Abraham: True godliness with contentment is itself great wealth.

Jesus: Those who live in the shelter of the Most High find rest in the shadow of the Almighty.

Lazarus: Wealth and shelter! Both mine! Because the Lord alone is my refuge. He is my God and I trust in him.

Abraham: Just open your eyes, and see how the wicked are punished. Evil doers will be the first to be led away as captives. Suddenly, all their parties will end.

Lazarus: Let all that I am praise the Lord. I will praise him as long as I live. I will sing praises to my God with my dying breath.

Jesus: *(To the audience...)* Lazarus the poor man did die. And he was carried by the angels to be with Abraham. *(Lazarus joins Abraham and Jesus. They put a white cloak around his shoulders)*

Lazarus: Our lives are in God's hands. He alone keeps our feet from stumbling.

Jesus: The rich man also died and was buried, and his soul went to the place of the dead. There, in torment, he saw Abraham in the far distance with Lazarus at his side.

Rich man: *(Far away, shouts...)* Father Abraham, have some pity! Send Lazarus over here to dip the tip of his finger in water and cool my tongue. I am in anguish in these flames.

Abraham: Son, remember that during your lifetime you had everything you wanted and Lazarus had nothing. So now he is here being comforted and you are in anguish. And besides, there is a great chasm separating us. No one can cross over to you from here, and no one can cross over to us from there.

Rich man: Please, Father Abraham, at least send him to my father's home. For I have five brothers and I want him to warn them so they don't end up in this place of torment.

Abraham: Moses and the prophets have warned them. Your brothers can read what they wrote.

Rich Man: No, Father Abraham! But if someone is sent to them from the dead, then they will repent of their sins and turn to God.

Abraham: If they won't listen to Moses and the prophets, they won't listen even if someone rises from the dead. *(To Jesus)* Will they, Lord?

Jesus: True. Unfortunately, it's true.

Jesus, Abraham and Lazarus exit together.

In the Shadow of His Wings

Psalm 18

Three Readers

#1: Refuge **#3:** Cover **#2:** Rest **#3:** Shelter
#1, 2, 3: Sanctuary
#3: Concealment
#2: Asylum for the sick **#3:** Immunity
#1: Help, relief, comfort **#2:** .In times of trouble
#1, 2, 3: Protection

#3: A sacred place
#2: A shelter for the homeless
#1: A tight battle formation

#1, 2, 3: *Verbal sigh. Pause.*

#1: I love you, God
#2: I love you, God
#3: I love you, God
#1, 2, 3: You are my strength
#1: You make me strong.

#2: God is the solid rock under my feet
#3: The only shining knight who can actually save me
#1: My God—into him I *run* for dear life

#1, 2, 3: I sing to a God
#2: Who is worthy of praise
#3: And find myself safe
#1, 2, 3: Safe
#1: And saved

[*Note: This list was written specifically for women in cross-cultural situations. It can be altered to suit the needs of different audiences.*]
#1: Cross-cultural meltdowns **#3:** Migraines **#2:** Language **#3:** Tension **#1:** Slander **#2:** Misunderstandings **#3:** Gossip **#1:** Monotony **#2:** Danger **#3:** Homesickness **#1:** I never do enough **#3:** There's too much to do **#2:** My husband ignores me **#1:** My parents aren't well **#2:** Its not safe here **#3:** I'm worried about my kids **#1:** I'm so lonely I could die **#2:** I feel guilty all the time
#1, 2, 3: And I don't know why!

#1: Desperation sweeps over me
#2: There's dark confusion over everything
#1: I'm terrified and uncertain
#2: In the face of many demons I shout,
#1, 2: "I will walk in the strength of the Lord God!"
#1: They screech at me
#2: They buffet me with their wings
#1: They whisper horrible curses into my mind
#2: My heart is in anguish
#3: Just trust in the Lord and everything will be fine
#1: Fear and trembling have overtaken me
#3: Just remember, God is in control
#2: Oh, that I had the wings of a dove, I would fly away and be at rest
#3: I'm sure it will all work out

#1: In my distress I cry out to the Lord God, my God
#2: Who desires truth **#3:** Touch **#1:** Intimacy **#2:** Honesty
#1: I tear my clothes **#2:** Fall to the ground **#3:** And lay it all before him

#1: *(Prays.)* O Abba, something is happening to me. My heart is dark, I can't see. Everything around me is falling apart. I can hardly see you. Will you help me, Abba? Will you take my hand?

#2: I cried to God to help me
#3: He heard me, *my* voice in *his* ears
#1: My cry brought me right into his presence

#3: And then

#1: He opened the heavens and came down. The earth quaked and trembled; the mountains shook. Smoke poured forth; fierce flames leaped, glowing coals flamed forth from him. He flew, soaring on the wings of the wind.

#2: The brilliance of his presence broke through, raining down. The Lord thundered from heaven; the Most High gave a mighty shout. His lightning flashed, and his enemies were greatly confused.

#3: He reached down from on high and took hold of me; he drew me out of deep waters; out of that ocean of hate, confusion, and self-doubt.

#1: He rescued me from the enemy chaos, from discouragement and the void in which I was drowning.

#2: My enemies hit me when I was down, but God stuck by me. He led me to a place of safety. I stood there saved—and surprised to be loved.
#3: God makes my life complete when I place all the pieces before him
#2: He gives me a fresh start **#1:** He lets me start over

#3: Refuge **#1:** Rest **#2:** Cover **#1:** Shelter
#1, 2, 3: Sanctuary
#3: Concealment
#2: Asylum for the sick **#3:** Immunity

#1: Help, relief, comfort **#2:** In times of trouble
#1, 2, 3: Protection

#2: A sacred place
#3: A shelter for the homeless
#1: A tight battle formation

#2: There are times when I need refuge, a place to run to
#3: I need to hide out and get my strength back
#1: In the safety of that place I remember that Jesus took the *only* storm that can take me under

#1, 2, 3: *Verbal sigh. Pause*

#1: I love you, GOD
#2: I love you, God
#3: I love you, God
#1, 2, 3: In you my soul takes refuge
#2: You make us strong

#1: Now that I'm put back together, I acknowledge what is not seen
#2: I'm alert to God's ways. I don't take God for granted
#3: Every day I review the way he works and try not to miss a lesson

#1, 2, 3: I'm standing on the rock in a wide open space

#3: God is a shield for *all* who look to him for protection
#1: Everyone who runs towards him—makes it
#2: That's why I'm praising his name, all over the world

Prayers from the Kingdom

Characters
President *(believer)*
Poor Man *(believer)*
Employee *(nonbeliever)*

Running time: 2-3 minutes

Setting
The Company President and Employee wear suits and are in offices next to each other (stage right and stage left). There is an invisible wall (or screen) between them. The Poor man is homeless. He is outside (downstage or off stage). In their separate spaces the characters do not hear or acknowledge each other.

President: *(Stands at "window". Prays.)* And thank you, Father, for this company that you helped me to create. Even in this difficult time you have allowed it to prosper. I'm so grateful for your generosity and grace. You are so merciful, Father!

Poor Man: *(Prays.)* Thank you, Father, that even in this difficult time you are always with me. You know what it's like to be poor. You always find a way to meet my needs. You are so merciful, Father!

President: I belong to *your* kingdom.

Poor Man: A kingdom so different from this world.

Employee: *(Talks to himself.)* Another day, another chance to prove myself! I finished the reports last night at home! The boss should be very impressed!

President: Help me, Father, to please you. I can't do anything without your help. All I have you've given me.

Poor Man: You've given me things that are far more real and permanent than anything this world has to offer.

Employee: Now, if I can just get that promotion my life will be perfect!

Poor Man: Thank you that every day you bring good out of evil. Thank you for the bread that never runs out!

Employee: And with it a raise! Finally! I'm sick of not being able to have what I want!

President: Now more than ever I know that nothing compares to knowing you.

Poor Man: All I want is more of you. You are my rock and my security.

Employee: I just want some security in this life. I never want to have to worry about money again.

President: Teach me how to succeed in your kingdom, the kingdom of heaven.

Employee: *(Looking out the window.)* Look at that beggar down there! That will never be me!

Faith and Drama

Poor Man: Thank you for teaching me courage.

President: Thank you for teaching me compassion and generosity.

Poor Man: Peace and joy.

President: Patience, gentleness, and kindness.

Poor Man: Thank you for adoption into your family.

President: For usefulness in your kingdom.

Poor Man: Sharing in your glory.

Employee: Once I buy a house I'll get married. Then I'll have everything I've always wanted!

President: Thank you for teaching me to put others first.

Employee: Once I'm the boss I won't be the one who has to worry anymore.

Poor Man: Because of your love, I'm free from fear.

Employee: I deserve it! I work hard. I'm a good person.

President: Because of you, I'm forgiven.

Employee: Finally, everyone will respect me.

President: You love me.

Poor Man: My honor is in your hands.

Employee: They'll envy me.

President: O, Father, to be a part of your family.

Poor Man: To be co-heirs with Christ.

Employee: That day will come. I'll make it happen.

Poor Man/President: To be a part of your Kingdom—now!

Employee: Then I'll finally be able to relax!

President: Thank you, Father. Your Kingdom come.

Poor Man: Your will be done.

Employee: And nobody better get in my way!

Poor Man: On earth as it is in heaven.

President/Poor Man: Amen.

President: *(Puts on his coat. Exits.)* John, I'll look at those reports when I get back. I'm only running out for a minute.

Employee: Yes sir!

President passes Poor Man, stops, gives him money.

Employee: *(Looks in his briefcase.)* Oh no! I left them at home! I can't believe it. I'm so stupid! Now I have to run home. This is a disaster! I'll take a cab, it'll be faster!

Walks down stage. Stands near Poor Man. Takes out his wallet and realizes he doesn't have enough money.

You've got to be kidding me! I spent my last dollar on lunch. Unbelievable! Now what? *(Starts to pace anxiously.)*

The Poor Man witnesses this. He walks up and hands the employee the money he has just received from the President.

Employee: *(Very surprised.)* What? Are you sure? I... oh well, okay. *(Takes it. As the Poor Man walks away the Employee mutters.)* He must be crazy! ...Taxi!

Exits as if going towards a cab.

Prophecies and Promises

Christmas

Four Readers

#4: Praise the Lord, all you nations. Praise him, all you people of the earth. For he loves us with unfailing love; the faithfulness of the Lord endures forever.

#3: For God so loved the world that he gave his one and only Son so that everyone who believes in him will not perish but have eternal life.

All: Love.

#2: It was prophesied: In love a throne will be established; in faithfulness a man will sit on it— one from the house of David.

#1: This is how God showed his love among us.

#3: He sent his one and only Son into the world that we might have life through him.

#4: And so the Word became flesh and made his dwelling among us.

#1: And we beheld his glory.

#2: The glory of the One and Only, who came from the Father.

#3: The true light that gives light to every man has come into the world.

#4: It was prophesied: The people walking in darkness have seen a great light; on those living in the land of the shadow of death a light has dawned.

All: Faithfulness.

#1: In love a throne will be established; in faithfulness a man will sit on it— one from the house of David.

#3: In the sixth month, God sent the angel Gabriel to Nazareth, a town in Galilee, to a virgin pledged to be married to a man named Joseph, a descendant of David. The virgin's name was Mary.

All: Righteousness.

#2: Mary was pledged to be married to Joseph, but before they came together, she was found to be with child through the Holy Spirit. Because Joseph her husband was a righteous man and did not want to expose her to public disgrace, he had in mind to divorce her quietly.

#4: But then the angel appeared to Joseph in a dream and said, "Joseph son of David, do not be afraid to take Mary home as your wife, because what is conceived in her is from the Holy Spirit."

All: The Holy Spirit.

#3: The angel answered, "The Holy Spirit will come upon you, and the power of the Most High will overshadow you, so the holy one to be born will be called the Son of God."

#2: "She will give birth to a son and you are to give him the name Jesus, because he will save his people from their sins."

#1: "For nothing is impossible with God."

All: Promises.

#4: It was promised: The Lord himself will give you a sign. The virgin will be with child and will give birth to a son, and will call him Immanuel—which means, "God with us."

#1: Of the increase of his government and peace there will be no end. The zeal of the Lord Almighty will accomplish this.

#3: For nothing is impossible with God.

#2: It was prophesied: For to us a child is born, to us a son is given, and the government will be on his shoulders. And he will be called Wonderful Counselor, Mighty God, Everlasting Father, Prince of Peace.

#4: If God is for us, who can be against us? He who did not spare his own Son, but gave him up for us all—how will he not also, along with him, graciously give us all things?

#1: Praise the Lord, for he loves us with unfailing love; the faithfulness of the Lord endures forever.

All: The King.

#2: Magi from the east came to Jerusalem and asked, "Where is the one who has been born king of the Jews? We saw his star in the east and have come to worship him."

#3: When King Herod heard this he was disturbed, and all Jerusalem with him. When he had called together all the people's chief priests and teachers of the law, he asked them where the Christ was to be born.

#4: "In Bethlehem in Judea," they replied.

#1: For it was prophesied: But you, Bethlehem, in the land of Judah, are by no means least among the rulers of Judah; for out of you will come a ruler who will be the shepherd of my people Israel.

All: The Shepherds.

#3: An angel of the Lord appeared to shepherds, and the glory of the Lord shone around them, and they were terrified.

#2: But the angel said to them,

#4: "Do not be afraid. I bring you good news of great joy that will be for all the people. Today in the town of David a Savior has been born to you; he is Christ the Lord."

#3: Suddenly a great company of the heavenly host appeared with the angel, praising God and saying,

All: "Glory to God in the highest, and on earth peace to men on whom his favor rests."

#4: But Mary treasured up all these things and pondered them in her heart.

#2: The angel had said, "You are to give him the name Jesus, because he will save his people from their sins."

All: Redemption.

#1: When the right time came, God sent his Son, born of a woman.

#3: God sent him to buy freedom for us who were slaves to the law, so that he could adopt us as his very own children.

#4: And because we are his children, God has sent the Spirit of his Son into our hearts, prompting us to call out,

All: "Abba, Father."

#1: Now you are no longer a slave but God's own child. And since you are his child, God has made you his heir.

#3: Praise the Lord, all you nations. Praise him, all you people of the earth. For he loves us with unfailing love; the faithfulness of the Lord endures forever.

All: Good News.

#2: It was prophesied about Jesus:

#1: The Lord has anointed me to preach good news to the poor.

#4: To comfort the brokenhearted.

#2: To proclaim freedom for those in bondage.

#3: To release prisoners from the darkness.

#1: To proclaim the time of *grace* has come.

#4: To comfort all who mourn.

#2: And to provide for those who grieve.

#3: Beauty for ashes.

Faith and Drama

#1: Gladness instead of mourning.

#4: Praise instead of despair.

#2: So praise the Lord, all you nations. Praise him, all you people of the earth. For he loves us with unfailing love; the faithfulness of the Lord endures forever.

#3: Because God so loved the world that he gave his one and only Son so that everyone who believes in him will not perish but have eternal life.

All: Amen!

Bible References
Isaiah 7, Isaiah 9:2-7, Isaiah 16:5, Isaiah 61:1-3, Jeremiah 31:3, Psalm 117, Matthew 1, John 1:1-9, John 3:16, John 14:27, Luke 1, Galatians 4:4-7, 1 John 4:7-12

O, Sovereign Lord

Four Readers

#1: Sovereign Lord, holy and true

#3: Lord, you are my God

#4: In perfect faithfulness you have done

#2: Wonderful things

#3: Things planned long ago

#1: The Sovereign Lord

#4: Will wipe away the tears from all faces

#2: He will remove his people's disgrace

#1: From all the earth

#4: You have been a refuge for the poor

#3: A resting place for the weary

#2: A shelter from the storm

#1: Shade from the heat, water in the desert

#4: Surely this is our God

#3: We trusted in him, and he saved us

#4: This is the Lord

#2: We trusted in him

#1: And he saved us

#3: All the days of my life were written in your book

#4: Every moment was revealed before one of them came to be

#3: You created my inmost being

#2: If I go up to the heavens, you are there

#1: If I go down to the grave, you are there

#4: If I ride on the wings of the morning

#3: If I settle on the far side of the sea

#2: Even there your hand will guide me

#4: Your right hand will hold me tight

#3: He said to me

#1: You are my servant, my glory and my splendor

#2: Do not be afraid, for I have ransomed you

#3: I, even I, am he who comforts you

#4: When you go through deep waters

#1: I will be with you

#3: When you go through rivers of difficulty

#2: You will not drown

#4: When you walk through the fire of oppression

#1: You will not be burned, the flames will not consume you

#3: For I am the Lord, your God

#2: The Holy One of Israel

#4: Your Savior

#1: I, even I, have ransomed you.

#3: Do not be afraid,

#1: No one can snatch you out of my hand

#2: No one can undo what I have done

#3: I have called you by name

#4: You are mine

#1: I say to the captives, come out

#3: And to those in darkness, be free

#2: *(Step forward)* You have searched me, Lord, and you know me

#4: You are familiar with all my ways

#1: Before a word is on my tongue you, Lord

#3: Know it completely

#4: You go ahead of me *(#1 moves in front of #4)* and behind me *(#2 moves behind #4. #3 is at the side of #4)* and you lay your hand on my head. *(#1,2,3 lay hands on #4's head. Pause.)* Such knowledge is too wonderful for me, too great for me to understand.

#1: Sovereign Lord, holy and true

#2: Lord, you are my God

#3: In perfect faithfulness you have done wonderful things

#4: Things planned long ago

#2: Before I was born you called me

#1: From my mother's womb

#4: You spoke my name

#3: The eternal God is our refuge

#2: And underneath are the everlasting arms

#1: The Sovereign Lord

#3: The faithful one

#4: Will wipe away the tears from all faces

#2: Surely this is our God

#1: We trusted in him, and he saved us

#3: This is the Lord

#2: Sing for joy, O heavens

#4: Rejoice, O earth

#2: Burst into song, O mountains

#1: For the Lord has comforted his people

#3: And will have compassion on them in their suffering

#2: He said to me

#4: See! *(All Readers drop their scripts and show the palms of their hands.)* I have engraved your name on the palms of my hands

---

Bible references

Psalm 139; Deuteronomy 33:27; Isaiah 25, Isaiah 43, Isaiah 49, Isaiah 51:12

The Shepherd King

Four Readers

Reader 1: The Sovereign Lord declares
Reader 2: You are my sheep
Reader 1: The sheep of my pasture
Reader 2: And I am your God

Readers 1, 2: The Shepherd King
Reader 2: The Lion and the Lamb

Reader 1: All we like sheep have gone astray
Reader 2: Each of us has turned to his own way

Reader 4: Sheep are stubborn animals
Reader 3: They're always getting hurt
Reader 4: They can't find food on their own
Reader 3: They can't defend themselves against predators
Reader 4: They're always getting lost
Reader 3: Sheep have to be looked after

Reader 2: There is no one who understands
Reader 1: There is no one who seeks God
Reader 2: All have turned away

Reader 3: The Bible refers to people as "sheep" 400 times

Reader 4: We look for leaders

Reader 2: A good leader loves the flock
Reader 1: And speaks the truth

Reader 4: A bad leader demands blind loyalty
Reader 3: A bad leader tries to control information

Reader 2: This is what the Sovereign Lord says
Reader 1: Woe to you shepherds who only take care of yourselves!
Reader 3: You eat well
Reader 4: Clothe yourselves with the wool
Reader 3: And slaughter the choice animals
Reader 2: But you do not take care of the flock

Reader 1: You do not care about the weak
Reader 2: Or heal the sick
Reader 1: Or treat the injured
Reader 2: You have not brought back the strays
Reader 1: Or searched for the lost

Reader 3: The people are scattered because there is no shepherd
Reader 4: No one searches for them, no one looks for them

Reader 3: This is what the Sovereign Lord says
Reader 4: I myself will search for my sheep and look after them
Reader 3: As a shepherd looks after his flock when he is with them
Reader 4: So will I look after my sheep
Readers 1, 2: I will rescue them

Readers 1: The Shepherd King!
Readers 2: The Lion and the Lamb!

Reader 3: God himself is coming!
Reader 4: He will come as a descendant of David
Reader 3: The great Shepherd
Reader 4: The Overseer of our souls

Reader 1: Sin is the predator of the sheep
Reader 2: Sin is crouching at the door
Reader 1: Its desire is to have us
Reader 3: Sin comes after us to deceive us
All Readers: To destroy us
Reader 4: And guilt follows us wherever we go

Reader 1, 2: No other shepherd will come between us and the sin that tries to devour us

Reader 2: The Sovereign Lord, our King
Reader 1: Tends his flock like a mighty shepherd

Reader 3, 4: No other shepherd will come between us and the sin that tries to devour us

Reader 2: He gathers us in his arms
Reader 1: He carries us close to his heart
Reader 2: He leads us with gentleness

Reader 1: Healing
Reader 2: Safety
Reader 3: Unfailing love
Reader 4: Rebirth

Readers 1, 2: The Shepherd King

Reader 1: He does not grow tired or weary
Reader 2: His understanding no one can grasp

Reader 3: He gives strength to the weary
Reader 4: And increases the power of the weak

Reader 2: Jesus said
Reader 1: I am the good shepherd
Reader 2: I know my sheep and my sheep know me
Reader 1: I lay down my life for the sheep

Readers 1, 2: The Lion and the Lamb

Reader 4: When the Son of Man comes in his glory
Reader 3: He will sit on his glorious throne
Reader 4: All the nations will be gathered before him
Reader 3: He will separate the people one from another
Reader 4: As a shepherd separates the sheep from the goats
Reader 3: He will put the sheep on his right and the goats on his left
Reader 4: Then the King will say to those on his right
Reader 3: Come, take your inheritance

Reader 1: For I was hungry and you gave me something to eat
Reader 2: I was thirsty and you gave me something to drink
Reader 1: I was a stranger and you invited me in
Reader 2: I needed clothes and you clothed me
Reader 1: I was sick and you looked after me
Reader 2: I was in prison and you came to visit me
Reader 1: For whatever you do for the least of these you do for me

Reader 4: Christ laid down his life for us
Reader 3: So that we may no longer live for ourselves

Reader 2: By his wounds we have been healed
Reader 1: We have returned to the Shepherd
Reader 2: And Overseer of our souls

Reader 3: Do not be afraid, little flock
Reader 4: It gives your Father great happiness to give you the Kingdom

All Readers: The Shepherd King! The Lion and the Lamb!

Reader 3: I saw a mighty angel proclaiming in a loud voice
Reader 4: Who is worthy to break the seals and open the scroll?
Reader 3: But no one in heaven or on earth or under the earth could open the scroll
Reader 4: Or even look inside it

Reader 1: I wept and wept
Reader 2: Because no one was found who was worthy to open the scroll

Reader 3: Then one of the elders said to me
Reader 4: Do not weep!
Reader 3: See, the Lion of the tribe of Judah, has triumphed
Reader 4: He is able to open the scroll and its seven seals

Reader 1: Then I saw a Lamb, looking as if it had been slain
Reader 2: Standing at the center of the Throne

Reader 3: For the Lamb at the center of the Throne is our Shepherd
Reader 1: He will lead us to springs of living water
Reader 2: And God will wipe away every tear from our eyes

All Readers: To him who sits on the Throne and to the Lamb
Be praise and honor and glory and power
For ever and ever!
Amen!

Bible references
Jeremiah 23:1-6; Matthew 25:31-43; John 10:1-6; Revelations 5:1-6

CPSIA information can be obtained
at www.ICGtesting.com
Printed in the USA
FSHW02n1844080518
47804FS